NORTH

MEDICINE GRIZZLY RANGE

MYTH VALLEY

MOUNT MARVEL

LARIAT

MYTH RANCH

LOST CANYON

WEST

Lyrico

Lyrico

THE ONLY HORSE
OF HIS KIND

· BY ·

Elizabeth Vincent Foster

· ILLUSTRATED BY ·

Joy Buba

The Parabola Children's Library
NEW YORK 1991

THE PARABOLA CHILDREN'S LIBRARY Edition, 1991
Originally published by Gambit Incorporated, Boston, 1970
Copyright © 1970 by Elizabeth Vincent Foster

LYRICO
The Parabola Children's Library / 1991

The Parabola Children's Library is a division of Parabola Books,
published by The Society for the Study of Myth and Tradition,
a not-for-profit organization devoted to the dissemination and
exploration of materials relating to myth, symbol, ritual, and art
of the great religious traditions. The Society also publishes
PARABOLA, *The Magazine of Myth and Tradition.*

Cover and book design by Trish Parcell
Design copyright by Parabola Books © 1991
Illustrations reproduced with the permission of Joy Buba,
courtesy of the Kerlan Children's Literature Research Collection,
University of Minnesota

ISBN: 0-930407-21-0

Parabola Books
656 Broadway
New York, N.Y. 10012

Manufactured in the United States of America

To
Mary Mathews and Frances Vance

Lyrico

One

Philippa had everything—dolls that walked, dolls that talked, dolls that drank out of a bottle and wet their pants, a doll house, a doll carriage, and trunks and trunks of doll clothes. She had enough stuffed animals to start a zoo. And besides that she had balls and jump ropes and roller skates and games and puzzles and paints and kits for making everything imaginable. And books, of course—a whole bookcase full. Philippa really had EVERYTHING.

Everything, that is, except the one thing in the world she wanted—and that was a HORSE.

Philippa lived in the top apartment of the tallest apartment house in the city. When her father started out in his business he had lived in a small apartment down near the street. But by working very hard he moved higher and higher until at last he was able to rent the large apartment at the very top, which had a wonderful view over the city and a garden on the roof.

"I do not mind working so hard," said Philippa's father, Mr. Pappadou, "because I am doing it to give my family everything—the best of everything."

Mrs. Pappadou said she did not really need everything and she wished Papa would not work so hard. But she did enjoy sitting on the roof.

"It is like living on a mountaintop," said Mrs. Pappadou, who had never seen a mountain.

What little time Mr. Pappadou took off from his business he spent growing rock plants in the garden on the roof, while Mrs. Pappadou did embroidery. She did beautiful embroidery. They would have been very happy if Philippa had been happy too.

But Philippa was miserable. She threw her dolls into corners without ever changing their pretty dresses or their wet pants. The only game she would play was a horse-race game; the only puzzle she would put together was called "Wild Mustangs"; the only pictures she would draw with her crayons and paints were pictures of horses (with flowing tails curled around to hide their hind legs, because hind legs are very hard to draw). And, of course, the only books she would read were *Black Beauty*, *Misty of Chincoteague*, and *Horsemanship for Young Riders*—books like that.

And the only one of her toy animals she would play with was a little wooden horse from Mexico with a real horsehair mane and tail, and a beautiful Mexican saddle

· 2 ·

that could be taken on and off. Mr. Pappadou's secretary, Miss Peregrine, had brought it to Philippa from her vacation in Mexico.

"You should give him a real Mexican name," said Miss Peregrine. "I rode a Mexican horse when I went to see a volcano on my vacation. His name was Parico—pronounced Pa-ree-co."

So Philippa named her little horse Parico, and called him Rico (pronounced Ree-co) for short. She spent hours saddling and unsaddling Rico, grooming his painted coat, and combing his flowing mane and tail. She pulled all the beds and sofas and the grand piano out of her doll house and made it into a stable for Rico. Mrs. Pappadou, who had taken a lot of trouble to furnish the doll house for Philippa with the very best doll furniture, felt sad about this.

"Please, Papa, buy me a horse—please, please, PLEASE!"

It made Mr. Pappadou very sad to have to say no to his little daughter—no, no, NO, about eighteen times a day. Of course he could afford to buy her a horse. It was not the expense.

"If we lived in the country it would be different," he explained, "but I absolutely must be near my business all the time. How could we keep a horse in the apartment?"

"Just a little one, a pony," insisted Philippa. "We can keep him on the roof. I'll take care of him every day, I promise."

"Dear, dear, dear, that is not a practical idea," sighed Mrs. Pappadou. "Mr. Jenkins, the janitor, would not like it. I am certain he would not like it. And those Van Pottles on the floor below would find something to complain about. No, Philippa, if you must have a pet, I will buy you a sweet little kitten, or some lovely goldfish."

But Philippa did not love the kitten, and after it had eaten the goldfish, it had to be given away to Mr. McLanahan for his little boy, who was home sick with whooping cough.

Mr. McLanahan was the doorman who stood downstairs in a dark green uniform with gold trimmings and "Metropolitan Towers" in gold letters on his cap. In spite of being so important, he was a friendly man and always had a word or a joke for people as they went in or out. But for Philippa he had something much better—stories about horses. Years ago Mr. McLanahan had helped take care of racehorses—real thoroughbred racehorses. He told Philippa about them while she waited for the bus that came to take her to school.

"The horses had the quality," he'd say. "They were the thoroughbreds, they were. It was the people was a low lot."

"Tell me about Thunderclap and the goat," said Philippa, who didn't care about the people.

So Mr. McLanahan would tell her about Thunderclap, a temperamental bay stallion who couldn't eat or sleep unless he had a goat named Clancy in the stall with him, and how Clancy had been stolen the night before a big race to upset Thunderclap so he wouldn't run fast the next day.

"Two o'clock in the morning the night before the

Sweepstakes," said Mr. McLanahan, "and there was Thunderclap weaving and fretting in his stall, refusin' his grain and his hay and getting no rest at all. I thought to myself, I know who the blackguards was that took Clancy and I have a shrewd notion what they done with him. So out I went and found him, and once Clancy was back in the stall, that horse calmed right down, et his feed, and slept like a baby. Horses is the queer creatures. Here's your bus, dear. Don't forget the books."

"Did Thunderclap win the race?" called Philippa as she ran across the sidewalk. She knew the answer, of course, but everyone wants the end of a story even if he's heard it before.

"He did! He beat Ace of Spades by half a length that day," shouted Mr. McLanahan as the bus rolled away.

Mr. McLanahan solved a big problem for Mrs. Pappadou. She was trying to find someone to stay with Philippa whenever she and Mr. Pappadou had to go out.

"There's my daughter Mary Carey, now," he said when Mrs. Pappadou asked him if he knew of a reliable sitter. "She's a harum-scarum kind of a girl in some ways, but she's got a good head on her and you can trust her to use it. Sure she'll be glad to help you out whenever you need her, Mrs. Pappadou."

So Mary Carey came in to stay with Philippa when Mr. and Mrs. Pappadou went out. And then, whenever she had the time, she took to helping Mrs. Pappadou with her housework. Mr. Pappadou insisted on buying every kind of labor-saving appliance as soon as it was invented, but they didn't save Mrs. Pappadou any labor because they made her so nervous she was afraid to use them. Mary Carey had very strong nerves, and anyway, she was interested in machines and enjoyed saving labor. Mary Carey said running Mrs. Pappadou's machines made a good fill-in job for her and she could always use the money. She and Philippa became great friends.

Mary Carey had red hair—not the carroty kind that frizzes but dark red and wavy.

"You'd be a sorrel horse if you were a horse," said Philippa.

"I'd be a strawberry roan," said Mary Carey, looking at her freckles ruefully in the mirror over the mantelpiece. Then she said: "Oh, well!" and stood on her head in the middle of the living room rug.

Mary Carey practiced whatever she was taking up at the time at the Pappadous', because she said there was more room there. "My outside interests," she called them. Mary Carey's outside interests were all interesting, and they all took up a great deal of room—acrobatics, ballet, judo, which is a Japanese way of stopping bad people when they come at you suddenly. All of these interests made a lot of thumping in the living room—the Van Pottles who lived downstairs were always complaining about it.

"What about that idiotic flea-size pooch they've got that yaps all day long?" said Mary Carey. "You're the one ought to complain, Mrs. P." But Mrs. Pappadou wasn't the complaining type.

Another reason Mary Carey practiced at the Pappadous' was that her father and mother didn't approve of her outside interests. They wanted her to stick to things you get paid for, like typing or hairdressing, both of which she had taken up at their request. But she said it killed her to sit still.

"And those women with their crazy hair, they drive me nuts," she said.

"So much energy!" sighed Mrs. Pappadou, who enjoyed sitting still.

But the best thing about Mary Carey—better than dancing on her toes or walking on her hands, or stopping a holdup man dead in his tracks (Philippa would be the holdup man)—the very best thing about Mary Carey was—she liked *horses*. That's putting it too mildly. She was just as crazy about horses as Philippa was.

"Why don't you take up riding for an outside interest instead of judo?" asked Philippa.

"Because I have a friend who gives me free judo lessons and I don't know anybody with a horse," said Mary Carey. "Except Mr. Kelly, the mounted policeman, and he won't let anybody ride Shamrock." And then she added: "Just my luck, my old man had to give up racehorses before I had a chance to get born! Shucks, I might be a jockey right this minute."

On evenings when Mr. and Mrs. Pappadou went out, Philippa and Mary Carey talked and thought and read about nothing but horses, horses, horses. If there were Westerns on TV, they watched them—not for the lost gold mine, or all that fighting in the bar, or the Indians, but for pintos and palominos, buckskins and blacks, bays, sorrels, appaloosas, saddle horses, stagecoach horses, teams driven by heroines at a mad gallop across the plains, Indian ponies, even packhorses and mules. A feast of horses.

"Oh, dear," Philippa sighed, "I wish I had that one, the one the sheriff is riding—isn't he beautiful, Mary Carey? Look at his tail!"

"Yeah, but that other guy's, the buckskin with the black mane and tail, boy, is that a pretty little mare!"

Then Mary Carey sighed, too.

"Would you like to have her on your ranch, Mary Carey?"

"I'll start with her!" said Mary Carey.

Mary Carey was saving up to go out West and marry a cowboy so she could live on a ranch and raise horses. They often talked about Mary Carey's ranch, and how Philippa would come out in the summers to help take care of the horses, especially the foals and colts.

"And I tell you what—you can choose any horse you want for you own," said Mary Carey. "You can choose a colt and break and train him yourself—any one you want, what do you say?"

So then Philippa thought hard—what kind of a horse would she choose?

"His name is going to be Rico," said Philippa, "but I can't decide what color he is going to be, or what kind of a horse."

"I'll have all kinds," said Mary Carey.

"I love palominos," Philippa said. "But a coal black Arab stallion with three white feet and a blaze on his nose, or a pinto—I love pintos. Couldn't I have two, Mary Carey?"

"No, sir. I can't afford to give away too many horses, for Pete's sake. Just one."

"Oh, dear," Philippa sighed, "it's so hard to decide what Rico will be."

"Perhaps you'd better not decide. Perhaps you'd better wait and see."

"I can't wait much longer, I just can't," said Philippa. "Haven't you saved up enough yet, Mary Carey?"

"I almost had enough last winter," said Mary Carey, "but then Mickey had to go and get appendicitis." Mickey was Mary Carey's little brother. He was always getting expensive things the matter with him.

"I think Rico will be a pinto," said Philippa, "a black and white stallion!"

After these talks with Mary Carey, Philippa dreamed that she was galloping over the plains on Rico, a glorious black and white stallion of her very own. Nobody could keep up with her. Her hair streamed in the wind. It was like flying!

When she woke up in the morning, there she would be, back in the apartment again, just the same as always, with her father ready to say No, No, NO, if she even mentioned horses. He didn't understand. Her mother didn't understand either. So Philippa would begin to feel sorry for herself, and that would make her cross, and that would make her mother begin to tell her what a lucky girl she was—why she had everything—EVERYTHING!—

and that would make Philippa crosser than ever, because what is the good of everything, if it isn't anything you want? Then Philippa would throw her toast on the rug, jam side down, and have a bang-up, knock-down, drag-out tantrum. Mr. Pappadou would hurriedly fold up his newspaper before he'd finished it and leave for the office, and Mrs. Pappadou would try to reason with Philippa gently, which made her even worse. Finally, the poor lady would go into her own room and shut the door, and tears would run down her nose onto her embroidery.

One Saturday Mary Carey came early and found all this going on.

"What's up?" cried Mary Carey. "What in tarnation is the matter with her?"

Philippa was lying on the floor, kicking holes in the wallpaper with both heels.

"The poor child is upset," said Mrs. Pappadou. "She would like to have a horse, but it would be difficult, almost impossible, to keep a horse in this apartment. It makes her very disappointed."

"Disappointed, my eye!" said Mary Carey. She took a glass of water off the breakfast table. "Get up!" she said.

From the way Mary Carey said this, Philippa knew that if she didn't get up, the water in that glass would come flying through the air smack into her face and run down her neck. There was ice in it. She got up.

"Come on, kid," said Mary Carey then in her usual cheerful voice. "Let's go into your room." So they went.

"Now, when I promised you a horse from my ranch," said Mary Carey, "I didn't know who I was dealing with.

No horse of mine is going to a spoiled, selfish brat, that's for sure! It takes good people to have good horses—patient people, strong people. How can you manage a clever, spunky young colt if you can't even manage your own temper! Believe me, you don't deserve a horse. No, you don't."

"Suppose," Mary Carey went on, "all this was in a book or on TV, who'd be the heroine in the story? A kid who had everything—best room in the house, best house in town, clothes enough for six ordinary kids, even her dolls got Italian hats. Her Dad works night and day and never takes a vacation, so he can give her the best. Her Mom worries all the time to keep Baby from fretting, and what does Baby do? Throws a fit because she can't have something that's impossible—right now, anyhow. Is Baby a good guy or a bad guy? What do you think?"

Philippa didn't say anything.

"Now I sure hate to go back on a promise," went on Mary Carey, "but, Juniper! I'm not giving any horses from my ranch to somebody who lets her own temper buck her right off in the mud. Suppose you had one of your fits and walloped that horse. It might plum ruin him. People have to have themselves well broke before they lay a hand on a horse. You've got to *deserve* a horse. And right now, young lady, I'd say you don't deserve a three-legged mule."

Philippa still didn't say anything. Then Mary Carey suddenly gave her a great big hug and said: "Come on, kid, we can't stay here palavering—we got work to do. There's some kind of a bigwig coming to dinner a week from Thursday. Your Ma's in a regular dither about it already. We got to get this joint polished up from the door-knob to the roof—especially the roof. Your Dad's going to have that rock garden manicured down to the last daisy."

"What's a bigwig?" asked Philippa. It was funny but she suddenly felt cheerful, as if she'd forgotten all about what had happened and what Mary Carey had been saying.

But she didn't forget. She didn't like the picture Mary Carey made of her. She could see that people wouldn't admire her in that picture—they might even think she was funny. Nobody likes to be funny except on purpose.

Philippa made up her mind she would be the kind of person who *deserves* a horse!

So in the week or so before Mr. Olympio came to din-ner, there was a change in Philippa. She never once asked her father to buy her a horse. She never once had a tantrum at breakfast. She picked up her toy animals and arranged them in a row, dressed her dolls, and even took the straw out of the doll house and put back the grand piano. She let her mother show her how to do cross-stitch, and she went out on the roof to see if she could help her father fix up the rock garden for Mr. Olympio.

Mr. Olympio was the bigwig who was coming to dinner.

"He's an important man—you could call him a world figure," said Mr. Pappadou. "Your grandfather knew him well in the old country. I have done business with him and his firm, but this is my first chance to meet him, the first time he has been in America. We must do him honor by having everything looking its best, especially my rock garden. In this garden are many flowers which grow on the high mountains of the old country, where Mr. Olympio has his famous country place. I think he will be pleased to find these campanulas falling over the rocks, and *Dianthus alpinus* and *Primula auricula*. He should feel at home."

"They're pretty," said Philippa, who had really never looked at them before, "but I wish they had easier names."

"Mountain flowers are the prettiest that grow," sighed Mr. Pappadou. "That is why, since I have no time to go to the mountains, I make my mountain here."

"Do you know what, you ought to take a vacation and go to some real mountains, Mr. Pappadou!" said Mary Carey, who was out on the roof emptying the electric broom. "You work too blamed hard, no kidding."

"I know. That's what Mama says, too," said Mr. Pappadou, sighing. "But it's impossible for me to get away from my business. My flowers I can enjoy right here. If I can keep them all happy I am happy!" He leaned over and picked off a wilted leaf. "My, this *Cyclamen europeum* is not so happy. It needs something, perhaps? But what I do not know. Now I must go to work. Goodbye, Philippa. Be‑happy, dear."

Philippa gave her father a big bear hug and said: "Sure!"

"You know, Mama," said Mr. Pappadou that evening

when they were getting ready for the great dinner for Mr. Olympio, "our Philippa is growing into a fine, good girl. She is very interested in my rock plants now. Do you see a change in her?"

"Yes, I do," said Mrs. Pappadou. "I was going to mention it to you. She has learned to do cross-stitch very well, and she is so sweet and cheerful. She hasn't mentioned a horse for over a week. Do you think she is quite well? I am a little worried."

"Now, Mama," laughed Mr. Pappadou. "She is growing up, that's all. I know that in her heart of hearts she still longs for her horse. But she does not mention it because she knows that it makes us sad to have to say always no. It is not easy to rule the heart's desire. I am proud of our daughter!"

Just then the doorbell rang.

"Oh my goodness!" cried Mrs. Pappadou. "That must be Mr. Olympio. He has arrived!" She hurried out into the hall to see if Mary Carey had put on the new lace apron and was answering the door.

It was a splendid dinner. Mrs. Pappadou had cooked her special dishes—the ones whose recipes, written on yellowed sheets of paper falling apart from much use, called for a list of strange ingredients which had to be bought in out-of-the-way little shops on the other side of town. They were simply delicious. Mary Carey waited on table like a real waitress. She remembered which side to pass things on, and never once put in her two cents' worth, as she called it, the way she usually did. Philippa wore her prettiest dress and in spite of having to use her best manners, she really enjoyed herself. As for Mr. Pappadou, he was bursting with pride and pleasure because Mr. Olympio took two helps of everything and seemed to be having an excellent time.

Philippa decided that Mr. Olympio didn't really look like Santa Claus. He had a long white beard, but his eyes behind his curly eyebrows were sharp and flashing, and you couldn't call him jolly. He was a little scary, in fact, with his booming voice and his look of knowing everything, but Philippa was fascinated by his talk with her father, even if she couldn't understand all of it. And when he told stories of the wild mountains far across the sea where his country place was, it was so interesting and exciting that Philippa couldn't bear the idea of going to bed. But when her mother said at last that it was bedtime, she got up from the table with never a word, kissed her father and mother, and made a little curtsey to Mr. Olympio.

"Good night, Mr. Olympio," she said, "thank you for telling such wonderful stories. I hope someday I can see your place in the mountains."

"Of course, of course!" boomed Mr. Olympio. "You and your father and your mother must visit me in the mountains. After this evening, this warm hospitality, we are friends, eh? We are like a family almost. Good night, little Philippa, good night."

"A charming girl, your daughter, a good girl," said Mr. Olympio after Philippa had gone to bed.

Mr. Pappadou was so proud and happy to hear Mr.

Olympio say this that he sat down and talked about Philippa for half an hour! He told Mr. Olympio all about how she had driven her parents almost crazy whining and teasing and having tantrums because she couldn't have a horse. And then how suddenly a little while ago she stopped, and now she was cheerful and helpful and easy to live with.

"Though I know she still secretly longs for a horse," said Mr. Pappadou.

"This is a fine little girl," said Mr. Olympio, "she has a loving heart. It is not easy to give up the habits of bad temper and self-pity. Such a little girl deserves a horse. Why do you not move to the country where she could have her heart's desire?"

"It is impossible," said Philippa's father with a sigh. "I *must* be near my business. In this country, to be successful, a man must work, work, work."

"Perhaps by working not so hard you might be even more successful in a different way," said Mr. Olympio. But Mr. Pappadou looked so pained at this that Mr. Olympio went on quickly: "I can see that you have been very successful, indeed. There can be few such homes as this in the city."

"There are none!" cried Mr. Pappadou. "Please, sir, let me show you around." So Mr. Pappadou showed his guest all over the apartment. In the kitchen Mr. Olympio admired the super-deluxe range and refrigerator, which were a beautiful shade of peacock blue, the dishwasher and clothes washer and dryer to match, and all the shiny machines for chopping and slicing and mixing and whipping and blending food that Mrs. Pappadou didn't know how to use.

"The meal you prepared with these ingenious devices was delectable," Mr. Olympio said to Mary Carey who was washing up.

"Shucks," said Mary Carey, "Mrs. Pappadou is the chief cook—I'm just the bottle-washer around here. She

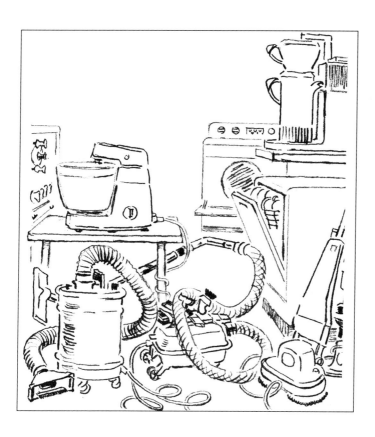

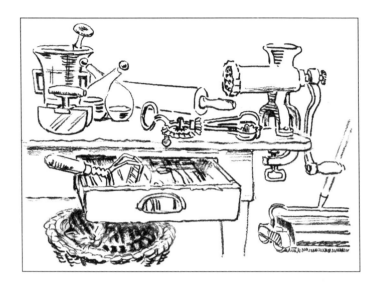

wouldn't touch an electric blender with a ten-foot pole, not even the automatic can opener. Does everything by hand. Machines make her terribly nervous."

"So!" said Mr. Olympio, raising his curly eyebrows. "However," he went on with a dignified bow, "I think you are over-modest, and I wish to thank you for your part in a memorable dinner."

Mary Carey was pleased. "That old-world courtesy you hear about," she told Philippa the next day. "He sure has the genuine article."

Mr. Pappadou took Mr. Olympio all over the apartment, and even insisted he take a peek into Philippa's room, where she was fast asleep. On a chair beside her bed stood the toy horse in a horse blanket she had made

for him. On the corner of the blanket she had cross-stitched his name: "Rico."

"What does that mean, 'Rico'?" asked Mr. Olympio, when they had tiptoed out again."

"That is the name of her toy horse, and of the real horse she dreams about," sighed Mr. Pappadou. "You see how she still longs for a horse, even though she says nothing about it."

"It is too bad. That little girl deserves her horse," said Mr. Olympio.

Poor Mr. Pappadou sighed again.

"Come, let me show you my garden," he said sadly and led the way to the roof.

When he switched on the lights, the little artificial waterfall sparkled as it fell over the rocks, and the flowers glowed with color.

"Beautiful!" boomed Mr. Olympio. "Beautiful! Why here I am at home! All these flowers—these crocuses and anemones—they are my friends, my neighbors in the mountains. It is a mountaintop, your roof. Here one can breathe, one can see the stars!" Mr. Pappadou switched off the lights, which made the stars show overhead. It was a cold spring night with a brisk wind from the west. The city with its light and noise and smoke seemed a long way down below.

Mr. Olympio walked all over the roof.

"Hm," he kept saying, "hm . . . hm." He seemed to be thinking. "Big enough—quite big enough," he remarked once, talking to himself.

"Yes," Mr. Pappadou said, "for the city, we have a good deal of space."

Then they went in, and Mr. Olympio sat and talked to Mr. and Mrs. Pappadou for a while.

"Allow me to say, Mrs. Pappadou, how much I admire your embroidery," he said. "I can see you are truly an artist."

Mrs. Pappadou was very pleased.

After they had a nice chat, Mr. Olympio left, thanking the Pappadous for a delightful evening.

"Tell your little Philippa," he said, "not to forget old Olympio. I will remember her, too. So now, goodbye, dear friends."

Two

Nothing happened after that for several weeks.

In all that time, Philippa never said *horse* once. What's more, she wasn't cross, and she didn't have a tantrum. Her father and mother, terribly relieved, didn't understand that the real reason she didn't talk about a horse was not because she no longer wanted one, but because she wanted one so badly. Parents often don't understand the real reasons. Philippa was determined to deserve a horse.

Then the rodeo came to town. Since Philippa had been so very good, her parents decided to let Mary Carey take her to see it.

"I'd rather she didn't go and see all those horses," said Mrs. Pappadou, "but we promised last year when she missed the rodeo on account of the mumps, so I do not see how we can say no now."

Philippa jumped up and down with joy and excitement. There would be lots and lots of horses—and what's more, there would be cowboys, real Western cowboys. It occurred to Philippa that if Mary Carey could just meet a cowboy right away, she could marry him and get settled on her ranch that much sooner. She didn't say anything to Mary Carey about this idea, but she gave it a lot of thought, especially the problem of how to meet the cowboy. If they could get close enough to one to talk to him, Philippa thought she could strike up an acquaintance by admiring his horse and then asking one or two questions which would show him she knew about horses. After that she could just say: "And this is my friend, Mary Carey, who loves horses, too, and who would be a wonderful help on a ranch"—something like that.

When Mary Carey came to get Philippa, she seemed uncheerful for a person on her way to a rodeo.

"You won't let Philippa eat too many of those awful things, will you, Mary Carey?" said Mrs. Pappadou, handing Mary Carey the carfare and the ticket and refreshment money. "What's the matter with you, dear? Don't you feel well?"

"Shucks," said Mary Carey. "I feel O.K. I'm just in the dumps about my brother's teeth."

"What did you say?"

"My kid brother has to have his teeth straightened."

"Oh well now, that is not so serious," said Mrs. Pappadou. "He will be much handsomer when he grows up, and it will not hurt him a bit."

"It may not hurt *him*, but it sure hurts me," said Mary Carey as she and Philippa went down in the elevator.

"How could it?" asked Philippa.

"Because I'm paying for it, that's why. There goes the Fund again."

"Oh no!" cried Philippa. "Oh *dear!*"

In the light of this misfortune, it seemed more important than ever for Mary Carey to meet a cowboy.

They got there early and they had wonderful seats in the third row, where they could see everything perfectly. In fact, they were almost too near for part of the show—Philippa felt sorry for the poor little calves being chased and roped and thrown and having their legs tied together, and the steers having their necks twisted so roughly. But Mary Carey thought they must be used to it by this time. There were clowns, too, like a circus, with a funny donkey that bucked them off, and when they landed on the ground there was a loud bang in the seat of their pants. And there were beautiful cowgirls in bright satin shirts and white leather chaps, who galloped around the ring picking up handkerchiefs from the ground and doing other daring tricks. Their horses wore bridles glittering with silver. Philippa decided to be a cowgirl when she grew up.

There were lots and lots of cowboys, too, of course. The ones who weren't performing stood around the gate where the calves and steers and bucking broncos came out, and from the special curl of their hat brims to the spurs on their high-heeled boots, they looked absolutely real—just like on TV. There they were—real live cowboys—each one undoubtedly with a ranch out West where he came from—but how to meet one?

It turned out to be quite a simple matter. In the intermission, people could go down and walk around where the horses were and look at them. And some of the cowboys were there, too. For once Philippa was more interested in people than in horses. There sat a handsome young man in a bright green shirt who had been one of the bucking-bronco riders. He was doing something to a saddle. Philippa walked right up to him.

"Hi," she said. She meant to go on and congratulate him on riding the bucking bronco and say she hoped it didn't hurt too much when he fell off, but after she said "Hi" she got stuck. Nothing more would come out. It was awful.

But the cowboy looked up and said "Hi," too. Then he smiled and asked her what her name was.

"Philippa," said Philippa.

"Enjoyin' the show, Philippa?" asked the cowboy.

"Oh, yes." Everything was going just as she had planned, and Philippa felt she had the situation in hand again now.

"This is Mary Carey," she said. The cowboy gave Mary Carey an even bigger smile than he'd given Philippa, put down his work, and stood up to shake hands.

"Hi'ya, Mary," he said, "I'm Bill Logan. Right pleased to make your acquaintance."

Philippa noticed that he made a lot of little wrinkles around his eyes when he smiled, and when he lifted his hat his forehead went back a long way toward the top of his head. He looked older than she had thought he was at first. But he was handsome just the same, and he seemed to like Mary Carey right away. But Mary Carey didn't smile back.

"I used to think all the good-looking girls was in Idaho," he said, "but since I went on the road I found out different. Travel sure is educational, Mary. Like they say, it broadens the mind."

Mary Carey pulled away her hand, which the cowboy was still shaking, and said it was time to go back to their seats.

"Now don't be in a rush," said the cowboy. "I won't let 'em start the show until you and me has had a chance to get acquainted. Come on, now. Don't run away until we've had a little chat."

"Where is your ranch, Mr. Logan?" asked Philippa, who wanted to get the little chat on the right track right away.

"Ranch?" The cowboy looked surprised. But before he could answer, one of the cowgirls, the head one, who had worn the purple hat, came calling and elbowing her way through the crowd. She had changed into a white hat now, and a white satin shirt sprinkled with glitter. Philippa noticed that near-to, her long hair was a peculiar shade of yellow, and some of her lipstick had come off on her big front teeth. She wasn't as beautiful as she had looked on horseback.

"Hey, Bill!" she was yelling. "Bill Logan, where's my saddle? We're on in five minutes, for Pete's sake. Ain't it fixed yet?"

"O.K., honey. Don't get in a sweat," said Bill. "It's fixed. Meet my friends, Ida. This is Philippa, and this here's Miss Carey. Girls, this is Idaho Ida, the Reckless Rider, Queen of the Rodeos from Calgary to Tucson. In private life she's Mrs. Bill Logan."

"Pleased to meet ya," said Idaho Ida, without looking up from the saddle, which she was examining critically.

"Philippa here wants to know whereabouts my ranch is," said Bill. Philippa didn't see why Ida should look at her with such a disgusted expression.

"What'd you tell her?" she said. "That it's the King Ranch in Texas, I hope. Well, I'll tell you where his ranch is, little girl. His ranch is at Wanzer's Trailer Park, outside Boise. Come on, Bill. You got three minutes to get the saddle on Bingo. Get along!"

"So long, girls," said Bill, shouldering the saddle. "Nice meeting you. Take care now . . ." A loud bell rang.

"We got to get back to our seats," said Mary Carey.

Philippa was still feeling disappointed when they got home. Everything had been going so well, and then the one cowboy she picked turned out to be married already! With Mary Carey's Out-West Fund wiped out by Mickey's crooked teeth, all hope of getting Mary Carey settled on a ranch that way was wiped out, too. And without Mary Carey's ranch, how could Philippa ever have a horse, her own horse, her dream horse, Rico?

Philippa felt that so much bad luck was a perfectly good reason for being cross, and she felt crossness beginning to grow inside her as they stepped out of the elevator and opened the front door. But before any of her crossness could spill out into the open, she saw something in the front hall that surprised her. It was a great big package, so big that it stood on the floor instead of on the table. And it was addressed to her!

Even Mrs. Pappadou didn't know what was in it.

"I can't imagine who would be sending you a package from Billings, Montana," she said. "We don't know anybody in Montana."

"Well, we won't find out by just standing looking at it," said Mary Carey. "Let's get a knife."

When she finally got it open, whatever it was was carefully packed in excelsior and cardboard and layers and layers of brown paper, and then tissue paper underneath, and it was tied down with thick twine. When Mary Carey got it loose and finally lifted it out of the box, it turned out to be—Philippa could hardly believe her eyes—the most beautiful handmade Western saddle embossed with flowers and curlycues and studded with silver. It wasn't very big—just about the right size for Philippa.

"OH!" was all Philippa co ld say.

"Is that a honey!" cried Mary Carey. "And look, Philippa, your initials are on it!" Sure enough, there were the letters *P.P.*, fancily carved inside a heart in the middle of the curlycues and roses.

"There's something else," cried Mary Carey rummaging in the bottom of the box. "Hey, look—a bridle!" She unwrapped a beautiful little bridle with embossed cheek straps and a fancy silver bit.

"Mr. Olympio!" exclaimed Mrs. Pappadou. "It must be from Mr. Olympio. Who else could have sent it?"

"That guy's a prince," said Mary Carey. "I knew it soon as I set eyes on him."

Philippa still couldn't say anything. She sat on the floor and stroked the beautiful saddle. Her own saddle, Rico's saddle. It was the most beautiful saddle in the world, and it was real. It was made of tough, smooth leather with a delicious leathery smell. It had a wide white girth to hold it on Rico's back. Rico would be real, too. Philippa felt suddenly sure.

When Mr. Pappadou came home, he was surprised.

"It's odd Mr. Olympio should do that," he said to Mrs. Pappadou. "I explained to him how impossible it is for us to give Philippa a horse. Now she will want one more than ever. I wish he had not sent the saddle."

"It has made her so happy!" sighed Mrs. Pappadou.

The next surprise was for Mr. Pappadou. He came home from the office with a notice from an express company.

"There is a box for me which has been sent air freight from abroad," he announced. "I make a guess that Mr. Olympio is sending me some plants for my rock garden. He showed great interest in my garden. How thoughtful and generous he is! I must notify Mr. Jenkins, the janitor, to have a man ready to help move this box onto the freight elevator. Mr. Jenkins, unfortunately, does not appreciate my garden. He complains about the heaviness of soil and rocks and never admires the beauty that grows from them."

"He's a crotchety old sour-puss," said Mary Carey.

The box came. It was certainly heavy. It had "Handle with Care" printed on it in five languages, and "Keep Watered" in seven, and there was a row of air holes along the sides at the top.

"That's for ventilation," explained Mr. Pappadou. "Plants need air just as people and animals do. And how thoughtful to put this cumbersome box on wheels." The box had a pair of wheels at one end so that it could be pulled along instead of lifted. It was like a small trailer. Even so, the men complained as they trundled it out of the elevator onto the roof. Mary Carey, who was helping as best she could, suddenly stopped in her tracks and stood still for a moment with an expression on her face as if she'd been hit on the head. Then she did a funny thing. She dashed indoors and in a moment she dashed out again, calling for Mr. Jenkins at the top of her voice.

"You're wanted in B basement, Mr. Jenkins. Al, too. They say it's an emergency! Please hurry!" The men, who were fiddling with the fasteners of the box, just about to open it, hastily departed.

"Oh dear!" cried Mr. Pappadou, "I'm so anxious to get those plants unpacked. They should be taken care of as soon as possible."

"I can open that box just as well as old Jenkins," said Mary Carey, "but the fact is, Mr. Pappadou, I dreamed up that emergency in B basement to get him out of the way.

I have a sneaking notion he'd better not be around when we open it. There's a noise in that box, Mr. Pappadou."

"A noise?" cried both Mr. and Mrs. Pappadou.

"What kind of a noise?" asked Philippa, suddenly more interested. She hadn't been too awfully excited about rock plants. "Maybe it's a bomb. Maybe crazy cranks sent it, and not Mr. Olympio at all!"

"Oh dear, oh dear!" cried Mrs. Pappadou, backing away from the box. But Mary Carey said not to worry.

"Don't call the FBI yet, folks. It isn't that kind of a noise."

Then suddenly they all heard it.

"It isn't!" cried Mrs. Pappadou.

"It can't be!" cried Mr. Pappadou.

"If it isn't, I'll eat my hat," said Mary Carey, prying at the box for all she was worth.

"Oh, hurry, hurry, HURRY!" gasped Philippa. "Open it, Mary Carey, open it quick—it WHINNIED!"

Mary Carey got the back of the box open—it was hinged at the bottom, and let down like a ramp. There was a thumping and clattering of hoofs, and out backed a small stocky horse—a pony really, but built like a horse, wearing a red horse blanket and a gold halter. Only its head and neck and legs and tail were visible because of the blanket, but that was enough to show that it was silvery gray and white—an unusual and striking pinto. Mary Carey put the lead-rope into Philippa's hand.

"Well, here he is," she said. "Goodness knows what we're going to do with him, but here he is!"

"Rico!" cried Philippa, and she threw her arms around

· 32 ·

his neck and buried her face in his thick, silky mane.

The little horse snorted and threw up his head, pushing Philippa away. Then he started across the roof, his hoofs tapping on the hard surface, dragging Philippa along as she held hard to the lead-rope.

"Help!" cried Philippa. "Whoa, Rico, whoa!"

But he went only as far as the fountain. There he plunged his nose into the water and drank in great long gulps.

"It's O.K., he's just thirsty," said Mary Carey. "His water pail is empty in spite of all those signs. Oh look, here's a letter tacked to the wall inside the box," she went on. "Directions maybe." She handed the envelope to Mr. Pappadou, who was just standing there, looking stunned.

"This cannot have happened!" he was muttering. "It cannot be true." The letter was addressed to him.

The little horse lifted his head from the pool and heaved a long sigh. Then he took another drink.

"Boy, was he thirsty!" said Mary Carey, coming over to where Philippa was standing holding the lead-rope. She patted the pony's neck. "So here he is. Rico—right out of the blue. And a pinto, just the way you wanted him. He's got a real pretty head, such a thick mane and pretty little ears. But—but," she stood back and looked at him critically, "there's something awful funny about his conformation."

"What's that?" asked Philippa, alarmed.

"His shape. He's a funny shape. Humpy, sort of."

There was no doubt that his back under the blanket looked queer.

"You don't think there's something wrong with him!" Philippa suddenly felt terribly worried.

"We'll take off the blanket and see," said Mary Carey, who felt worried too, and she started to unbuckle the blanket.

"In this letter," said Mr. Pappadou, "Mr. Olympia states that this horse is not like other horses. It belongs to a rare breed, extremely rare, and . . ."

"OH!" cried Mary Carey and Philippa together.

The blanket was off. There stood the little horse, a handsomely marked silver-gray and white pinto. The extraordinary thing about him, the unbelievable, wonderful thing was—HE HAD WINGS! Beautiful pearly wings growing from his shoulders and folded back against his sides. He raised them and shook them a little and settled them back into place, as if it were a relief to get rid of the blanket.

"Oh!" they all cried again.

The little horse raised his head and looked around, his sharp ears pricked, nostrils wide, looking intently in one direction. Then with a nervous snort he swung around and stood staring the other way. Every move, every attitude of his strongly arched neck and elegant head, his smooth quarters and clean sturdy legs, made him look like a picture or a statue, a dream of glorious horsiness. His wings didn't seem out of place; they belonged to him and added to his wonder.

Presently, lowering his head, he started off across the roof again, nearly pulling the lead-rope out of Philippa's hands.

"Whoa!" cried Philippa in a panic. But when he reached the nearest flower bed, he stopped and very daintily began to crop Mr. Pappadou's *Phlox subulata* Emerald Cushion Blue.

"Oh no, you mustn't," cried Philippa, pulling on the rope. But to her surprise her father said: "He's hungry. Let him eat."

Mrs. Pappadou, who had been speechless, at last found words.

"What a beautiful, beautiful creature!"

"The first thing we must do is read the letter," announced Mr. Pappadou. "Listen carefully."

My dear friend Pappadou:

You are surprised and perhaps upset that I should send a horse for your little Philippa when you have decided that it is impossible for her to have one. But please read what I have to say before you judge me too severely.

I quite agree that your luxurious home is ill suited for keeping an ordinary horse. But this horse is quite different from ordinary horses, and is, I believe, well adapted to your situation. These little animals—a small subspecies of the rare pegasidae *—are now limited to a narrow range in our most inaccessible mountains. Full grown, they are, as you can imagine, almost impossible to capture alive, and on the rare occasions when an adult specimen has been taken, it has proved completely untamable. But once in a while, on some precarious ledge among the highest peaks, a native hunter succeeds* in cornering a foal too young to fly, and brings it home to his children. Great is then the rejoicing, for these animals can, at this age, be trained as safe mounts for children, and they are, moreover, believed to bring great good luck to their owners. Since there is another strongly held belief that a curse will fall on anyone who sells or steals one of them, they are never seen in zoos or circuses. Indeed, any stranger coming to our mountains with the purpose of collecting these horses would do so at the peril of his life.

Because I am such an old resident, and have sometimes been able to do certain favors for my mountain neighbors, this little stallion was presented to me in a touching ceremony on my return from America. I was deeply moved, for this gift is the most precious one these simple people can bestow. But the fact is that I cannot keep a horse, especially one so small it could not possibly carry me. (Were it one of the larger breed, the type pegasidae, I could make good use of it, but those noble animals are now, alas, unobtainable, if not extinct.) I am away too much on business to give this little creature the care and affection it should have, so it occurred to me that here is a horse which Philippa could keep with very little trouble on your city mountaintop.

Do not be afraid that because he is a stallion he will be wild or unmanageable. He has a very gentle disposition, and as long as you do not remove the halter he now wears, you will find him docile and well broken. As for feeding, he lives entirely on alpine flowers, and for his size you will be surprised at how little he eats.

And do not fear for your plants, my good friend Pappadou. Use the stable litter to fertilize your garden beds and you will see a magical result. Your little horse will more than make up for the flowers he eats, this I can assure you.

One thing more—and here is the reason I presumed to act without first writing for your permission—if now, or at any time in the future, you decide you do not want this horse, all you need to do is take off his halter. While he wears his halter he is tame and obedient; without it he turns wild as an eagle. The homing instinct in these animals is highly developed and their endurance is very great. Take off the halter, and he can fly back to his native mountains from anywhere in the world.

So now I hope you will forgive me, my friend. And I hope Philippa will be happy with Lyrico. Lyrico, I forgot to mention, is the animal's name—it struck me as a happy coincidence.

With warmest regards,
Z. Olympio

"Oh, but I wanted to name him myself," cried Philippa, "I wanted to call him . . ."

"Rico," said Mary Carey. "Well, he's already called Rico—short for Lyrico, don't you see? That's what Mr. Olympio called a coincidence."

"Rico!" cried Philippa. "Oh, Rico!" and she buried her face in Rico's horsey-smelling mane. Rico pushed his head

against her shoulder and rubbed it up and down a couple of times as if his ear itched. Then he went back to nibbling at the flowers, delicately picking out one here and one there with his flexible velvet lip.

"Just be sure he doesn't rub the halter off when he does that," cautioned Mr. Pappadou.

"He seems as gentle as he is beautiful," said Mrs. Pappadou. "But do be careful just the same, dear!"

And so Philippa had a horse.

Three

Now began the most wonderful time!

Philippa spent every minute she wasn't in school or asleep out on the roof with Rico. She would have slept on the roof, too, only her mother wouldn't let her.

At first she held the lead-rope while Rico grazed, but soon Mary Carey thought it would be safe to tether him if someone stayed near, and after a while they even dared to turn him loose. He always came as soon as he was called.

"My lease for this apartment does not say anything about not keeping a horse," said Mr. Pappadou, "but I think it would be wiser if we didn't mention that we have one."

"You're not kidding," said Mary Carey. "That old

Jenkins the janitor just snoops around looking for things to yak about! And as for the Van Pottles down on the forty-eighth, complaining is the best thing they know how to do . . . But look, Mr. Pappadou, I think we ought to tell my Dad. He'd be a big help. There isn't a thing about taking care of horses he doesn't know, and he can keep a secret, don't worry."

"An excellent idea!" said Mr. Pappadou.

So Mr. McLanahan came up. And after he'd got over his surprise at seeing Rico, and had felt his legs and looked at his teeth, he was terribly enthusiastic.

"Sound as a dollar!" he exclaimed. "And looks to be a clever little pony, too, in spite of the wings, which is something I never saw on a horse before, nor even dreamt of. But otherwise he's the ideal mount for the little girl, sir. And if it's true what you say, that turning him out on these flowers here, without hay or grain, will keep him fit—why, I see no problem with his care whatever."

The big crate Rico had come in, painted up, with a roof to shed the rain, made a good stall. It also made a good trailer after Mr. Pappadou had some heavy-duty wheels and tires put on it, and a hitch installed on his station wagon. He found he could take the trailer down in the freight elevator, hitch it to his station wagon in the garage in the basement, and use it to haul plants and bales of peat moss from the nursery in the suburbs where he bought his supplies. He told Jenkins the janitor that the peat moss was for his flowers. It was, too, but not until after it had been used for bedding in Rico's stall.

"If you ask me," grumbled Jenkins the janitor, sniffing,

"he hauls something stronger than peat moss in that there contraption." A trailer that's used for a stall can't help smelling a little horsey.

"What's the harm if the gentleman wants to put some good fertilizer to his plants?" asked Mr. McLanahan. "There's nothing sweeter than horse manure for the garden."

What actually happened when Mr. Pappadou put Rico's stable manure on his rock plants was just what Mr. Olympio said it would be—nothing short of magic! Almost at once the plants began to grow twice as fast as before, with flowers twice as big and three times as bright. They spread all over the roof until there was scarcely room to walk between the banks of color. What Rico ate could hardly be noticed.

The saddle fitted perfectly. Rico would raise his wings out of the way while he was being saddled, and when Philippa was getting on. Then he would settle them back into place, covering her legs with silky feathers.

"It may be hot in summer," Philippa said, "but it feels good now." The weather was bright and cool and blowy. The air, for city air, smelled fresh.

Mr. McLanahan came in his time off and gave Philippa riding lessons. There was a path all around the roof between the flower beds—not much room. "But it's nearly the size of a small ring," said Mr. McLanahan, "big enough to begin in." He taught Philippa always to mount on the left side of the horse. "The left side is the right side—remember that, now," he said. "It's called the *near* side—like you'd say 'my horse has lost a shoe behind on the near side'—that means his left hind foot, you understand."

"Yes," said Philippa, "but my horse doesn't wear shoes."

"Never mind that, he has a near hind foot just the same. The other side is called the *off* side. Do you have that, now?"

"Yes, yes," said Philippa. "How do I make him canter?"

"Easy, easy!" said Mr. McLanahan. "The place to begin is at the beginning! Though to tell the truth," he went on, "I don't know the first thing about riding on one of these heathen out-West saddles. And as for riding a pony that's half airplane, I don't know that either. But never mind, if you learn to stay on his back and keep a light hand on the rein, the way you won't ruin his mouth, the fine points can come later. Now!"

Soon Philippa was riding Rico around and around the roof by herself. She learned to post when he trotted instead of going bump, bump, bump, and, though there scarcely was room, she even cantered for a few steps. She learned that the way to stay on is to grip with your knees, not hold on to the pommel or steady yourself by the reins. The reins should be loose (but not too loose), except when she wanted to steer Rico, or stop him, and even then she should not pull too hard or long, or shake the reins or jerk them.

"A light hand on the reins, always," said Mr. McLanahan. " 'Tis the mark of a good horseman."

"Do you really think it is safe for her to ride alone, Mr. McLanahan?" asked Mrs. Pappadou anxiously.

"The way she catches on to the hang of it, Madam," said Mr. McLanahan, "I wouldn't be anxious. And for all he's a stallion, the pony seems safe and quiet enough."

But just the same, Mrs. Pappadou told Mary Carey to be sure and stay out on the roof when Philippa was riding.

One day when Mrs. Pappadou was out, Mary Carey was on the roof watching Philippa ride round and round. In the middle of the roof was a sort of little house—or at least it looked like a house. It really was the top of the elevator shaft. At first Mary Carey used to walk all the way around behind Rico so she never lost sight of Philippa when she went behind the elevator shaft, but by now that no longer seemed necessary, and Mary Carey just waited by the door to the kitchen until Philippa came round. In fact, at one point Mary Carey stepped into the kitchen a moment to check the clothes washer. It was a good thing she did, because suddenly the service door opened, and in walked Mr. Jenkins the janitor.

"I'm going out on the roof," he said gruffly.

Mary Carey thought fast.

"Oh, Mr. Jenkins," she said. "You're just the person we've been wanting to see. Won't you please look at the drain under the kitchen sink. It doesn't seem to be draining right."

"No time now," said Mr. Jenkins.

"Oh please!" begged Mary Carey, "just *look* at it. You always know what ought to be done."

"What ought to be done is call the plumber," said Mr. Jenkins testily, but he did lean down and open the doors under the sink.

Mary Carey turned and ran out on to the roof to warn Philippa.

"Quick, quick!" she panted. "Mr. Jenkins is coming. Get Rico out of sight!"

Alas, there was no time to dismount, lead Rico into the stall, and close the door. The only hope was to hide him behind the elevator shaft. Maybe the janitor would not go around to the other side.

"Oh!" gasped Philippa. "Quick, Rico," and she dug her heels into Rico's flank. He bounded out of sight around the elevator shaft.

The next moment Mr. Jenkins was there. "Ain't nothing wrong that I can see," he growled. "You don't have to run like that, Mary Carey McLanahan. I ain't going to bite you." Then he laughed his disagreeable laugh.

"What was it you wanted to see on the roof, Mr. Jenkins?" said Mary Carey politely, though she didn't feel polite.

The janitor didn't answer. He looked around sourly at the mounds and carpets of blue and white and yellow and pink flowers.

"Stinking mess!" he snorted. "Management oughtn't to allow it." Then, to Mary Carey's horror, he started to walk around the elevator shaft.

"Where are you going?" cried Mary Carey.

"I'll do my job, you mind your own," snapped Mr.

Jenkins. She couldn't stop him.

"Oh gosh, the game's up this time," thought Mary Carey desperately. "Once he sees Rico, it's all over. Oh, poor Philippa."

Mr. Jenkins rounded the corner, Mary Carey at his heels.

There was no one there!

The janitor leaned over and pulled up a handful of Carpathian bluebells.

"Blocking the vent!" he grunted. Then he walked to the other side of the shaft, and with one more disgusted look around, went away.

Mary Carey couldn't believe her eyes. Where was Philippa? Where was Rico? She felt frantic with worry. She dashed around the shaft again, calling and shouting as loud as she could. There wasn't any answer. Philippa and Rico were not there. They just weren't on the roof.

But where could they be?

Mary Carey looked at the parapet around the outside of the roof. It was four and a half feet high. They couldn't have fallen over—they just *couldn't!* She thought of the dizzy drop on the other side of that parapet—forty-nine floors to the street, so far down that cars and buses looked like crawling bugs, and the roar of traffic was no more than a faraway hum.

"What'll I do!" she cried. "What in the world am I going to do?"

At that moment a shadow blotted out the sun, there was a whoosh and a gust of wind, and then the familiar clop, clop of hoofs on the hard roof. Mary Carey looked up. There stood Rico folding his wings, and there on his back sat Philippa.

"Oh, Mary Carey," cried Philippa joyfully. "What do you think we did? We *flew!* I've learned how—look!" And before Mary Carey could collect her wits, Philippa turned Rico, prancing and excited now, raised the reins, touched her heel to his flank, and leaned forward in the saddle. Rico didn't need to be urged. He broke into a canter and took off six feet from the parapet, cleared it like a showhorse, and in another moment his silvery wings were fully spread, and he and Philippa were airborne. They circled twice around the roof, gaining altitude fast, then swooped down again to a graceful landing beside Mary Carey.

"It's wonderful," glowed Philippa. "Oh, Mary Carey, it's the most wonderful thing in the world!"

"Glory be!" gasped Mary Carey, sinking into a wheelbarrow and fanning herself with a seed catalogue that happened to be in it. "You scared the living daylights out of me. What do you think your Ma is going to say? You better break it gently!"

They broke it gently. First Mr. Pappadou had a private showing. When he was at last convinced that Philippa could manage Rico perfectly, both on takeoff and landing, and that she wouldn't fall off (just to be sure, he had a safety belt made so she *couldn't* fall off)—they finally invited Mrs. Pappadou to come up and see Rico's new trick.

"Show Mama," said Mr. Pappadou, when they were all gathered on the roof, "show how Rico can jump."

"Oh no! Jumping is very dangerous," cried Mrs. Pappadou in alarm.

"Shucks!" said Mary Carey. "She's been jumping for a week. Prettiest thing you ever saw."

Philippa turned Rico toward a hurdle Mary Carey had set up with the mop handle laid across two chairs. As always when he was going to take off, Rico was excited. He pranced and fidgeted with the bit, tossing his head impatiently. Philippa held him back, firmly but gently, until he was in position. On his first jump he did no more than clear the hurdle smartly, as any pony might do. The second time he raised his wings and took a long skimming glide over the mop handle.

"Oh goodness! Oh my *goodness!*" exclaimed Mrs. Pappadou. But after the third jump Rico never landed at all. Wings wide, he soared and flapped into the air over the roof and flew in circles over their heads, while Philippa laughed and waved to her mother.

Mrs. Pappadou almost fainted.

"I cannot allow it. I will never allow it. My nerves will not stand it," cried Mrs. Pappadou as soon as she could get her breath.

But finally, after many arguments and many demonstrations to prove how safe it was, she reluctantly agreed to allow Philippa to fly. She must not land except on her own roof; she must always be home in plenty of time for supper; she must keep away from the airport for fear of being run into by a plane. A mother can think up all kinds of rules and conditions. Philippa promised. She

would do anything, if only she could fly.

"I envy you so much I could cry," said Mary Carey. Mary Carey was much too big and heavy to ride Rico. "He'd crash before he took off if I even tried," she said ruefully.

"It's too bad you had to grow up," sympathized Philippa. "Flying Rico is the most wonderful thing in the world. It's like a dream, only better—much, much better!"

"Well, enjoy it while you can, kid," said Mary Carey. "One of these days you'll grow up yourself, I shouldn't wonder."

"Oh I hope not!" cried Philippa. It was an awful thought.

Four

The weather had been good for weeks, and it still held—bright and cool, with a fresh northwest breeze, just right for flying. Philippa had the most glorious rides. She circled above the city, keeping well up to avoid attracting attention. As a matter of fact, Mary Carey said that Rico's silver and white coloring was a sort of camouflage— that and his pearly blue-gray wings broke up his shape so that from below he didn't look like a horse, and with so many things flying around—helicopters and jets, not to mention sea gulls and starlings and pigeons and kites—he was scarcely noticeable in the sky.

Philippa soon learned how to put Rico through all his paces: to soar, bank, and climb, dive and zoom ahead at maximum speed. Of course she had no speedometer. But one day they met a hawk wheeling in midair (it was an osprey which happened to be migrating over the city) and they chased it for fun. The hawk got away, but Rico kept right on its tail for the first few minutes. Hawks are about the fastest birds that fly. When it finally pulled away from them, Philippa looked down and saw with dismay that they were over the airport, which she'd promised to keep well away from.

"Heavens, Rico, we've got to get away from here fast," she cried, pulling him into a short turn and streaking for home. Fortunately Rico, like all horses, could always find the way home. The city looked so different from the air that Philippa might easily have got lost, even though her apartment house, being the tallest in the city, stood well above most other buildings. But of course there were the downtown towers, much higher, that stuck up like granite peaks into the sky.

It was from one of these towers that the trouble started.

The day after the hawk chase Mr. Pappadou put down his morning paper, looking quite serious.

"Where did you go on Rico yesterday, Philippa?" he asked.

"Well, I accidentally got a little near the airport," said Philippa. "I didn't mean to, and there weren't any planes around at all, so it wasn't a bit dangerous. I'm awfully sorry, Papa."

Mr. Pappadou looked even more serious.

"It says here," he said, taking the paper up again and

reading something from the first page, "'An unidentified signal which appeared yesterday on the radar screen at Winterbottom International Airport has puzzled air authorities in this city. General Blitz, Commander of the Rougemont Airforce Base, denies the possibility that a foreign plane could have reached the city undetected. Suggestions that it might have been a UFO have been discounted by Dr. Eugene Hydrogen, Professor of Astrophysics at the State University. "Poppy-cock," the Professor is quoted as saying . . .'"

"Oh dear," worried Mrs. Pappadou, "has she done anything against the law?"

"What law? There isn't any law against flying around on a horse," said Mr. Pappadou. "You'll just have to be more careful, that's all, Philippa. Don't go *anywhere* near the airport!"

"Yes, I won't," promised Philippa. "I mean, no, I will . . . Anyhow, Rico and I will be terribly careful. We promise."

"It is good to see her so happy," sighed Mrs. Pappadou, "and I love little Rico, but I must confess I get very, very nervous."

No further news items appeared in the paper about the mysterious signal.

But two days later on the editorial page there was a letter from a man who said he had seen something which might bear on the unexplained radar signal reported at the airport.

"I work on the sixty-third floor of the Twenty-first Century Building," he wrote. "Last Tuesday at 4:36 P.M.,

I happened to be looking out the window of my office, when a light-colored object in the sky caught my attention. It was moving rapidly in the direction of the airport. It was too small for an aircraft, and much too large for a bird, though it appeared to have wings. It disappeared so fast that I had no time to observe it carefully. The idea flashed through my mind that it might be one of those flying saucers you hear about so much nowadays, but I didn't mention it to anybody (except my wife, of course) for fear of being laughed at. But I did make a note of the time, and since it corresponds exactly with the time of the radar blip, I decided to report what I had seen."

"You'd better keep well away from those skyscrapers, too," said Mr. Pappadou to Philippa.

During the next few days the papers printed other letters from people who had seen a mysterious object. Some of them said it was like a one-man helicopter, others that it looked like a boat under full sail, and one report stated flatly that it was saucer-shaped with blinking lights and a full crew of little green men in bubble helmets. The Bird-Watchers' Club held a special meeting to evaluate reports of a huge bird, probably a California condor (which would be a new record for the state), or even a roc, formerly resident of Arabia, but for several centuries thought to be extinct. An ornithologist from the Natural History Museum applied for permission to shoot the specimen for the Museum collections, but pressure from the S.P.C.A. got the permission denied. The Air Force warned pilots to watch out for an Unidentified Flying Object over the city, and the Mayor issued a statement saying that City Hall had everything under control and the public should not worry.

But Mr. Pappadou did worry. He felt sure that Philippa's daily rides on Rico were beginning to be risky, but he didn't have the heart to forbid them altogether. He didn't know what to do.

Then the weather changed, and the change cut down on reports of mysterious flying objects, but it brought new and much more serious worries to the Pappadou household.

"What's the matter, Rico?" said Mary Carey one day. "Don't you feel hungry?" Rico was nosing the flowers listlessly, scarcely nibbling a bite.

"Try these," urged Mary Carey, moving him to a different spot. But Rico wouldn't eat.

"I don't think he likes this muggy weather," said Philippa. "I don't like it either. It's so hot and sticky, and the air smells bad."

"If I were you, kid, I wouldn't go too far today," said Mary Carey. "Just take a few turns over the roof and see if Rico won't work up an appetite. Besides, the visibility's so bad you might get lost."

"Rico would never get lost, never!" protested Philippa. "Not even in this horrible smog. But I feel like Rico, I haven't any pep either." So she took just a short ride. Even so, Rico was quite winded when he landed. His flanks heaved as if he'd been racing, and he stood with hanging head and drooping wings while Philippa unsaddled him.

"I don't like it, Dad," Mary Carey told her father that evening. "I wish you'd go up and have a look at Rico."

Mr. McLanahan came the next day. He looked Rico all over. Then he shook his head.

"I can't find anything special wrong," he said, "but he does look poorly. Off his feed, I guess. It's no doubt this humid weather. When it clears up in a day or two he'll be his own self again, I shouldn't wonder."

But it didn't clear up. It only got hotter and muggier and smellier. The air felt thick and choking. From the Pappadou's roof there was nothing visible but dirty gray murk.

Then the flowers began to wilt. Brave little plants that could grow in a thimbleful of soil in the crack of a mountain precipice, baking in the summer sun, freezing in winter storms, languished in this poisoned city air. They turned limp and brown and sickly. Poor Mr. Pappadou did everything he could think of to save them, but still they drooped.

"It's terrible to lose my plants," he told Mrs. Pappadou, "but what are we going to do about Rico? The flowers are all he can eat—his life depends on them."

"I know, I know," cried Mrs. Pappadou, wringing her hands. "Poor Rico, he looks so sick. His wings hang down, and his coat doesn't shine anymore. His ribs are beginning to show. I don't know what Philippa will do if anything happens to Rico!"

"It is very worrying," said Mr. Pappadou. "But there is only one thing we can do if this goes on. We must take the halter off and let him go. Philippa must see that we have no choice."

"Her heart will break!" cried Mrs. Pappadou.

Then suddenly the weather got better. It rained all one night, clearing up bright and cool in the morning with a fresh breeze from the west. It was Saturday. Mary Carey came early and she and Philippa led Rico out of his stall to let him feed. He seemed to feel better and he grazed on the few flowers that remained with a better appetite then he had shown in a long time. When Mary Carey offered him a bunch of violets she'd bought at a florist's, he ate a few of them, too.

"That's good," said Mary Carey. "That shows we've something to fall back on if the rock plants give out entirely. Might get to be expensive, of course."

"Expensive doesn't matter," said Philippa, "only Rico matters."

Then she gave Rico an extra good grooming, as if brushing his coat and combing his mane and tail would make him feel better.

"I think he does feel better," she said when she had finished. "Don't you think a little exercise, just around the roof, would be good for him, Mary Carey?"

"I don't suppose it would do any harm, but take it easy," cautioned Mary Carey. "Now I better get going with the vacuum," and she went into the house.

Philippa saddled Rico, mounted and walked him around the roof. The wind ruffled Rico's silky mane which Philippa had combed out so carefully. The air felt fresh; the sun sparkled; the horizon, for the first time in weeks, was a hard, clean line.

"Such a *beautiful* day!" thought Philippa. It was the best kind of a day for flying. Why not? Rico would surely enjoy stretching his wings for a bit after being grounded for such a long time. She turned his head toward the parapet and touched his flank with her heel. Rico took off.

It was glorious—simply glorious to be in the air again. Philippa felt made of joy. She felt like urging Rico up, up, up toward the sun so they could zoom down, down, down in a wonderful dizzy dive, or streaking away at top speed like the day they chased the hawk. But of course that wouldn't be right. She mustn't ride Rico too hard until he was back in condition again. A short flight must be absolutely all for today. And so, after about five minutes, Philippa turned Rico toward home.

Not until then did she realize that they had lost a good deal of altitude. Usually they kept high above the apartment, dropping down to land on the roof. But now, as the apartment building loomed ahead of them, Philippa saw that they were below the level of the roof; in fact, they were barely skimming the tops of much lower buildings.

"Oh my goodness, Rico," said Philippa, "up, up, up!" and she raised the reins, her signal for going higher.

Rico responded with an effort that took them up a few feet.

"Come on, boy," urged Philippa, "up higher, boy."

But Rico didn't go higher. His wings beat slowly, unsteadily. His breathing was labored.

"What's the matter, Rico?" Philippa began to be worried.

They were nearly home now, but they were coming in much, much too low. Five or six stories of the apartment house towered above them. Each apartment had a sort of balcony terrace on the side they were approaching. People would be out there on a day like this. They would see Rico!

"Try, Rico!" pleaded Philippa.

Then suddenly, for the first time, Philippa felt frightened to be in the air. She glanced down at the street below and a cold shiver went through her. Rico was faltering. What if he fell? Philippa grabbed the pommel and froze in the saddle. Her head reeled.

Rico struggled on toward the building, losing altitude fast in the last stretch. But he made it. He landed with a bump on the terrace of the apartment of Mr. Eric Gundersen, an engineer for the Vacuum Tube Transportation Corporation, who was away in Biloxi on business. But of course Philippa didn't know this. By this time she would have been glad to see anybody, and she hoped the orange curtains which were drawn across the glass doors to the terrace would open and somebody would come out. What if they saw Rico? Philippa was too terrified to care.

Rico stood trembling with exhaustion, his flanks heaving, his breath coming in great sobbing gasps. His coat was dark with sweat. Philippa knocked desperately on the doors, but no one answered. What was she to do?

Gradually Rico's breathing got easier. His legs stopped shaking. He lifted his head, gave himself a great rattling shake, and settled his drooping wings into place.

"Good Rico," Philippa patted his neck. "Poor Rico. It's all my fault. I never, never should have made you fly. But what are we going to do now? Oh dear, I wish we were home!" Philippa didn't want to cry. She banged as hard as she could with both fists on the doors again, but it was no good. No one came. Listening, Philippa could hear the roar of traffic from the street below—the sound of a million people. Yet here she and Rico were, desperately alone—as alone as they would be on a ledge of the far wild mountains where Rico came from. What's more, Philippa realized with a sinking heart, here, as it would be in the mountains, there was only one way to get away: they would have to fly. Philippa thought of the comfortable push-button elevator, just a few feet inside these doors, which could whisk her home in a few moments. Instead of that she must take off into the air again over that dizzy drop, and hope Rico would have the strength to carry her to safety. The idea was terrifying, but there was nothing else to do.

Rico was moving around restlessly now. He seemed to be O.K. Philippa ran her hand under the girth to see if it was tight. Then she screwed up her courage, mounted, and fastened her safety belt with care. She didn't want to think about what she was going to do, or she might never have the nerve to do it.

"Now, Rico," she said.

Horses have a way of knowing, somehow, what their riders are thinking, and especially what they are feeling. Whether Philippa's panic communicated itself to Rico that way, or what happened, is hard to say. But in any case he did something he had never done before. He refused. That means he started to jump and then stopped in the middle. Philippa was thrown forward with a jerk. If it hadn't been for the safety belt, she might have catapulted over the wall into space. Having a horse refuse to jump is upsetting even on solid ground. Thirty-seven stories up in the air it completely destroyed Philippa's nerve. If her life depended on it—and perhaps it did—she would not face that jump again.

But now Rico took matters into his own hands. Backing up as far as he could, he gathered himself together, and before Philippa knew what was happening, he bounded forward and cleared the railing somehow, ticking badly with his off hind hoof. For a sickening moment Philippa thought they were falling. Then Rico's wings spread out and held him in a glide. As they swept past a corner of the building, a strong updraft sent them soaring up four stories without moving a wing. Philippa's courage soared too. Now they were almost level with the roof. They were almost home.

But here they met a head wind. Ordinarily, with a few strong strokes Rico would have gained altitude, circled, and landed into the wind as prettily and precisely as a bird. But now, though it really wasn't blowing very hard, the wind seemed too strong for him. As he labored against it he lost altitude, and Philippa saw with dismay that they were still below the roof; that they were not going to make it; that they would be lucky if they reached the terrace of the apartment below.

In another moment Rico landed with a clatter outside the open French doors of Mrs. Van Pottle's living room, where a subcommittee of the Ladies' Reform League was having a morning coffee.

Bibi, Mrs. Van Pottle's toy poodle, was out on the terrace trying to warn the world that danger was approaching—at least he thought it was danger—but his frantic squeaks were drowned out by the discussion of the Ladies' League. When the danger suddenly dropped out of the sky almost on top of him, Bibi gave a terrified yip and dashed into the house, where he had hysterics under the sofa.

Bibi wasn't the only one. Ladies screamed and dropped their cups of coffee. Danish pastries flew in all directions, chairs tipped over, vases crashed. The hubbub scared Rico out of his wits. With a startled snort, he leaped over the terrace rail, summoned every ounce of strength, and flapped his way up to the roof, where he landed panting and exhausted, but safe at last.

Five

"Heavens to Betsy!" cried Mary Carey, "Where have you been? I've been worried silly about you! What's the matter with Rico? Philippa, what happened? You look awful! Tell me, what happened?"

"They saw us," gasped Philippa, sliding off unsteadily. "I couldn't help it. Rico is sick, he can hardly fly. We had to land at the Van Pottles', and it was full of ladies, and they saw us! Oh, what are we going to do, Mary Carey? They'll tell Mr. Jenkins and he'll make us get rid of Rico—I'll just die!" Philippa threw her arms around Rico's neck and began to cry.

Mary Carey stood perfectly still while she took in this

dreadful news. She had to think, and she had to think fast. For two whole minutes, the only sound was Rico's heaving breathing and Philippa's sobs.

"O.K.!" said Mary Carey suddenly. "I've got it. No time for tears now, honey. Just lead Rico into his stall. Quick! Never mind the saddle. We've got to get him away from here before they come to look for him, and he can't fly, that's for sure. Put him in and close the door while I talk to your mother and telephone your Pa."

In a matter of minutes, Rico was in his trailer and the trailer was in the service elevator on its way to the garage. The two handymen who always helped hitch the trailer to Mr. Pappadou's station wagon huffed and puffed.

"What you got in there, for Pete's sake," grumbled one of the men, "rocks?"

"Yes, of course," said Mary Carey. "Mr. Pappadou is switching to a new kind of rocks imported from Czecho-slovakia. His plants need something ordinary American rocks haven't got."

Philippa kept her eyes on the ground. She kept praying under her breath: "Oh Rico, don't whinny! Don't, don't, DON'T!"

The handymen looked at each other and winked. They thought Mr. Pappadou was crazy to have a rock garden at all, so Mary Carey's crazy reason didn't surprise them in the least.

It seemed to Philippa that it took the men a hundred years to hitch the trailer onto the station wagon. But at last one of them said, "O.K., McLanahan, haul 'er away!" And they started.

As Mary Carey drove cautiously up the ramp and out into the street, a loud bell clanged in the garage and a voice over the intercom called all building employees to report to the janitor's office.

"Emergency!! Come at once!" The handymen, who thought they deserved a cup of coffee after moving that trailer full of rocks, went grumbling upstairs.

As Mary Carey stopped for a light at the end of their block, a siren sounded ahead of them, and pretty soon a police car flashed past.

"Hmm . . ." said Mary Carey. "Do you suppose . . . ?" She switched on the radio, and a rock-and-roll tune filled the car as they threaded their way through the traffic. The traffic was bad. It took them a long time to reach the expressway that led to the superhighway that led to the interchange that led to Route 404 where the Green Thumb Nursery was. They finally got to the interchange, but there they were stuck for several minutes in an underpass, and the radio went dead. When they came out again, the music had stopped and a voice was giving a news bulletin.

". . . to remain calm," said the voice. "The Mayor further stated that the FBI has been notified and is working closely with local police to clear up the mystery . . . Professor Max Blau, noted authority on UFO's, is on his way here from Miami Beach to take part in the investigation. This is station WBNK, your instant news station. Stand by for a further report on this amazing incident . . ."

"What's he talking about?" asked Philippa.

"You, I think," said Mary Carey, as the voice began again.

"Here's Ray Hawkins, reporter from the *Daily Standard*, bringing you an exclusive interview with one of the witnesses, recorded a few minutes ago at Metropolitan Towers, scene of the reported incident. Mr. Hawkins . . . "

"Metropolitan Towers! That's our apartment house," cried Philippa.

"I told you," said Mary Carey. "Now listen."

A different voice was talking now: "Please tell us, Mrs. Van Pottle, just what happened. From the very beginning, please."

"Oh, it was terrible! I'm still very upset. It's hard for me to collect my wits."

"Always was," commented Mary Carey, and this time Philippa said "Shh."

"Where were you when the incident occurred, Ma'am?"

"Why, I was in the living room. We were all in the living room. There was a meeting of the League. We were discussing . . . I don't even remember what we were discussing. This has been a very severe shock. Very."

"Yes, Ma'am. Just tell us what happened," urged the reporter.

"Well, the first thing that happened, my little dog Bibi started barking. Bibi's such an alert little watchdog, you know. He sensed that something unearthly and awful was about to happen. And all of a sudden, it happened!"

"What happened?"

"What? Why, it was an object—one of those outer space things. With wings. It flew right onto the terrace outside the French doors. It had men in it, too. I distinctly saw one. Don't ask me to describe them. They were rather small and green, and had bushy hair. I'm sure they had some kind of invisible electric ray that paralyzes people. We were all completely paralyzed!"

"What did you do?"

"Do? We couldn't do anything. We were paralyzed, I tell you . . . Then suddenly it took off again and I called the police—the police and the janitor and the Mayor and all the newspapers. I should have called the President, too. It's time people in authority paid some attention to this problem!"

"Green! She thought I was a little green man with bushy hair! Oh goodness!" Philippa giggled. "Invisible electric rays—is that what she said? Oh dear, oh *dear*, how funny!"

"Well, it's funny, but it isn't so funny, too," said Mary Carey grimly. "We've still got problems."

Philippa stopped laughing. She remembered poor Rico in the trailer behind them.

"Do you suppose Rico is all right? What are we going to do when we get to the nursery?"

"Well, the first thing we have to do is unload him and see."

As they drew up in front of the nursery, Mr. Greene, the proprietor, waved to them.

"Mr. Pappadou telephoned," he said. "He asked me to let you keep a pony here for a while. He says it eats alpines and he'll pay for what it eats. That's a sort of expensive pony to keep, ain't it? Eighty-five cents a plant, three for two-fifty."

"He doesn't eat much," said Philippa.

"Well," said Mr. Greene, "most of the alpines that are in bloom now are out back of the greenhouse. You can drive right around this way."

Rico, when they unloaded him, stood with hanging head. His coat, under the blanket which hid his wings, was all rough with dried sweat. So Mary Carey found an empty shed where they could take the blanket off without being seen, and they unsaddled him and gave him a good grooming. After that, and after he'd had a long drink, they led him out to where all sorts of rock plants were blooming in rows in small raised beds. Listlessly Rico nibbled a few blue ones labeled: "C. *carpatica*, special strain."

"He doesn't seem hungry," said Mr. Greene, who had come out to see what was going on. "Why the blanket? He looks all bundled up. Shouldn't think he'd need it in this weather."

"He's sick," said Mary Carey. "The vet said to keep it on." This was the first time they had to explain Rico's blanket, but it wasn't the last. They were to repeat this little story about a thousand times in the next week.

What a long, dull, worried afternoon they spent out behind Mr. Greene's greenhouse! Part of the time Rico stood still, so lifeless and miserable that Philippa could hardly bear to look at him. Then he would move about restlessly, pulling Philippa after him by the lead-rope. Time and again she led him to the campanulas, but he only nosed them, or at most nibbled one or two.

The sun sank lower and lower.

"Where can Papa be?" Philippa worried.

"He'll come, never fear," Mary Carey assured her. "You know how hard it is for him to get away from business, even on a Saturday afternoon."

Philippa looked at every car that drove up to the nursery, expecting her father would get out of it, but the people who did were always strangers.

Finally, long after sunset, when even Mary Carey was beginning to feel sort of discouraged, a taxicab roared up and came straight around to where Mary Carey and Philippa and Rico were huddled.

"There they are! Stop, stop here, driver!"

"Oh Papa," cried Philippa. "And oh Mama, you're here too! We thought you'd never, never come!"

"We thought we'd never, never get here," said Mrs. Pappadou, getting out of the taxi with her arms full of packages. "My poor little girl!" She gave Philippa a big hug, dropping packages right and left.

"Are you all right, dear? How is Rico?"

"He won't eat enough," said Philippa.

Mr. Pappadou and the taxi driver were unloading mountains of luggage out of the taxi and piling it beside the station wagon.

"Whatever's in all those bundles and suitcases, Papa?" asked Philippa.

"I'll explain later," said Mr. Pappadou. "You and Mary Carey load Rico."

They put Rico into the trailer and fastened the door.

There was room for the saddle and bridle up front.

Mr. Pappadou took a luggage rack out of the taxi and he and the taxi driver strapped it to the roof of the station wagon. Then they filled it with bundles and laced a tarpaulin over the whole thing.

"Put the back seat down," said Mr. Pappadou. "Now, Mama—" Mrs. Pappadou took the paper off the two big round packages which seemed to contain quilts. She spread these side by side in the back of the station wagon.

"Let's see, where did I put the pillows?" said Mrs. Pappadou, rummaging around.

"*Sleeping bags!*" cried Mary Carey. "Oh Mr. Pappadou, you're going to take a vacation at last. Isn't that just great! Philippa, if you're not the lucky kid. Gee . . . " Mary Carey looked wistfully at the loaded car and the sleeping bags spread out so cozily in the back.

"What do you mean, Mary Carey? Papa, what? Are we going on a trip? Are we really, Papa?"

Mr. Pappadou nodded his head.

"What happens to my business I just don't know!"

"Since we have to go West for poor Rico's sake," said Mrs. Pappadou, "let us go and forget our other troubles."

"West?" cried Mary Carey. "You mean you are going West? You mean *real* West, OUT West? Oh gosh all hemlock!"

"You don't like the West, Mary Carey?" Mrs. Pappadou was surprised.

"Like it! Oh-h-h-h . . . " and Mary Carey did what

she had never done before: she burst into tears.

Of course Philippa understood.

"Oh Papa, oh Mama—can't Mary Carey come, too? Oh please, please, please. She wants to . . . She's always wanted to. She was going on the Fund, but then Mickey had to have his stupid old teeth straightened . . ."

"Why, of course Mary Carey is coming!" exclaimed Mrs. Pappadou. "How could we possibly go without her? I asked Mr. McLanahan if he thought she would be willing to come. He thought she would, so her brother Michael brought her things in a small suitcase. It's in the car somewhere—we'll find it later, dear."

"Willing!" Mary Carey stood perfectly still for a long moment while her face changed from misery to one big grin. Then she grabbed Philippa and whirled her around with her feet off the ground.

"Yippee," cried Mary Carey, and letting go of Philippa, she did three cartwheels one after another.

"My goodness!" said Mrs. Pappadou.

Six

They drove all night. Philippa and Mary Carey were to sleep in the sleeping bags in the back, and Mr. Pappadou would wake Mary Carey for a turn at driving when he got too tired.

They bought sandwiches for supper, and while they ate, Mary Carey and Philippa heard what happened at the apartment after they left.

"The police came," said Mrs. Pappadou. "They said witnesses had seen a flying saucer land on our roof and they insisted on searching the whole place. I was very nervous. But then your Papa came home and of course they found nothing. I hate to imagine what would have happened, Mary Carey, if you had not thought so quickly how to get Rico out of the way."

"Your Mama and I had been talking for some time about Rico," said Mr. Pappadou. "He was not doing well, and we felt we were wrong to keep him in the city. But we did not think he was strong enough now to fly home if we took off the halter and let him go. We had almost decided to take him to the mountains to get him into condition for the long flight, when all this happened. Now, suddenly, here we are on our way! Fortunately, I had already made some arrangements."

"We packed in such a hurry," said Mrs. Pappadou. "I probably forgot more than I remembered. I'm not even sure I put in my embroidery."

"It occurred to me we could not stay in motels with Rico," added Mr. Pappadou. "So on our way out of town I stopped at a camping store and asked the man for a complete camping outfit for four. 'I have only ten minutes,' I said, 'please hurry!' I don't even know what he gave me, but there's a great deal of it."

"Oh boy!" said Mary Carey. "Camping!"

Philippa couldn't go to sleep for a long time. As the car whirred along through the dark, the rumbling of the trailer kept her worrying about poor Rico, back there all alone. She hoped and prayed he was all right.

"When we get to the mountains," she kept thinking, "Rico will get well again." But the mountains were a long, long way off. Finally Philippa must have gone to sleep because she never heard Mary Carey get up to take her turn at driving.

When she woke up, the car had stopped. It was dark and very quiet, and cold air that smelled sweet was blowing in through the open door of the station wagon. Philippa sat up, wondering where she was, and what had happened. Somebody was moving back by the trailer, dim figures in the glow of a flashlight. Was something wrong with Rico?

They had Rico out of the trailer by the time Philippa had scrambled out, barefoot in the cold dew.

"We've got to let him rest a little," explained Mary Carey. "It will be morning soon. We'll take the blanket off so he can stretch his wings while it's still dark."

Rico walked around, nosing the grass. There were buttercups and daisies and clover under the beams of the flashlight, but Rico would not eat them. Presently, head down and feet close together, he bent his front knees, folded his hind legs, and lay down with a sigh.

"Poor Rico!" said Philippa.

"We'll never get him to the mountains if he won't eat," said Mary Carey. "We'll have to buy him some flowers."

So after a rest they went on to the next large town they came to, to look for a florist.

"Why sure," said a man with a lunch pail, whom they stopped to ask. "Blumengartner, he's a florist down on South Main Street, but he won't be open yet." The man looked as if he thought it was a funny thing for tourists with a horse trailer to want to buy flowers at seven o'clock in the morning.

They had breakfast while they waited for Blumengartner's to open. Then they bought a large bunch of violets and some carnations. Rico would not look at the carnations, but he did nibble a few violets.

By early afternoon both Mary Carey and Mr. Pappadou were so sleepy they simply could not go on driving. When they saw a sign that said "State Park, Two Miles" they turned off the highway, and soon they were parked in a campsite under some pines.

The first thing they did was to unload Rico, water him, give him more violets, which had been kept fresh in a pail, and tie him to a tree in the shade. Then they all four spread out sleeping bags on the ground beside the car and went to sleep. They were exhausted.

They woke up again in a few hours when people began to arrive and set up camp all around them. In no time at all every campsite was taken. There were big tents and little tents, pup tents, cruiser tents, balloon tents, Sahib Safari tents, and every other kind in all the colors of the rainbow. There were station wagons with awnings, microbuses with screened porches, land cruisers with picture windows, camping bodies on pickup trucks—sleeping two, four, or six, and every kind of travel-trailer from homemade to super-deluxe with shower baths and air-conditioning.

All the tents and campers and trailers had radios, and some of them had television. In no time at all folding chairs were set out in front of each camp, fathers were sitting in them listening to the evening news, mothers were busy getting supper, and children were racing around whooping and shouting and working off energy after sitting all day in the back seats of cars.

"Jeepers!" said Mary Carey, putting her hands over her ears.

Philippa stood by Rico saying "No, no, NO!" to crowds of children who wanted a ride.

A man whose two little boys were pestering Philippa with questions about the pony—What was his name? Why did he wear a blanket? Why couldn't they have a ride?—got into conversation with Mr. Pappadou.

"Great to get out here in the woods, isn't it?" he said. "Like I tell the Missus, a man's got to get away from the pressures of modern life, back to nature, so to speak, and forget his worries. Otherwise he'll go nuts, right?"

Mr. Pappadou, who had hardly ever been so worried in his life, said he agreed.

"Did you read in the paper," said the man, "where a UFO landed on a building right in the middle of the city? Eyewitnesses said the thing had like flashing lights— you know, the regular kind. But then others swore it was more of a horse with wings, with a little green man riding on it. Funny thing, isn't it?"

"I read something of the sort," said Mr. Pappadou coldly. "But I don't believe everything I see in the papers."

"Yeah, that's right, too," said the man. "But these witnesses . . . makes you wonder . . ."

They had cold baked beans and warm lemonade for supper, because Mrs. Pappadou wouldn't use the Kookqwik stove Mr. Pappadou had bought at the camping goods store.

"It's the best and very safest kind," insisted Mr. Pappadou, "the man said so. Let Mary Carey cook supper on it, Mama."

But Mrs. Pappadou was sure it would blow up.

"If the girls will just gather some firewood," she urged, "I can cook our supper on this nice fireplace here. I've always wanted to try cooking over an open fire." But Mary Carey and Philippa couldn't find a single scrap of firewood. The campsite and all the woods around it had been stripped of every twig.

"The man in charge says there's a firewood pedlar who comes around, but he's been," Mary Carey reported, "and it's against the rules to gather firewood anyway, even if there was any."

They were too tired and discouraged to care.

"We'll go to sleep early and start before daylight," said Mr. Pappadou.

They didn't get to sleep very early. There was too much noise. But even so, long before the sun was up next morning, they had coaxed Rico into eating the rest of the violets, loaded him into the trailer, and were speeding West again.

Afterwards, when Philippa thought about the trip, it was like somebody flashing slides, all jerky and out of focus, on a big screen: hills, trees, billboards, cities, gas stations; hot dinners in restaurants, camp breakfasts at chilly dawns; then bigger farms, smaller towns, fewer billboards, telegraph wires looping along beside the highway,

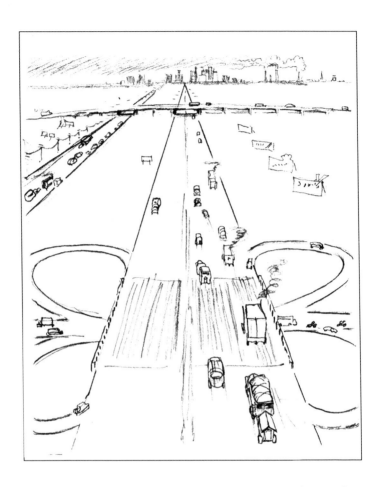

fences rising and dipping with it, while the land grew flatter and flatter and the sky wider and wider, until neither looked as if it would ever end.

All the fun and adventure there would have been for all of them in this tremendous trip was drained away by worry about Rico. They didn't talk about it, but one dreadful question never left their minds: would they get there in time? Would they win the race to the mountains in time to save Rico?

Rico grew weaker and weaker. The further they went, the harder it was to buy flowers for him.

"Violets? Well, no. They're out of season just now, dearie. But we have a special on carnations this week, only two dollars a dozen for these lovely red ones."

"But Rico won't eat carnations!" Philippa would exclaim in despair, and the florist would look at her sharply and say: "What did you say, dearie?"

At camping places and wherever they stopped to take Rico out for a rest, the children were a problem. "A pony! a pony!" the cry would go up, and in a minute a crowd of kids were flocking around asking questions and begging for a ride, holding lumps of sugar and handfuls of grass under Rico's nose. He was getting no rest. Philippa scolded and ordered and stamped her foot, but it did no good. Finally Mary Carey came to the rescue.

"I wouldn't go near the pony if I were you," she would say in a good loud voice, "that pony has hippotoxicosis, and it may be catching." Some father or mother would hear her, and in a twinkling there wouldn't be a child in sight.

"What's that?" Philippa was surprised.

"Well, it's a little invention of my own," said Mary Carey. "It sounds bad, and it seems to work." It worked every time.

Rico's round quarters were creased and gaunt now; his hip stuck out like a jagged rock; every rib showed through his lusterless coat. Worst of all, when they took off the blanket, his lovely wings hung down all limp and untidy.

"I could cry just to look at him," Mrs. Pappadou told Mr. Pappadou. But she kept saying to Philippa that they would soon be in the mountains and then Rico would quickly get well.

They could not travel so fast now because they had to stop oftener to let Rico rest. When they took him out of the trailer he could hardly walk, and usually he lay down almost at once. Mr. Pappadou kept searching the roadside for new flowers, but only once in a while would Rico eat one of them.

It was hot. It kept getting hotter.

"It's hotter than a boiler room," said Mr. Pappadou.

"It's hotter than an oven," said Mrs. Pappadou.

"It's hotter than hinges," said Mary Carey.

"Why are hinges so hot?" asked Philippa. But she was too sticky and thirsty and discouraged to care.

It was time to pull out beside the road for a rest, though the place was dusty and full of cans and papers, and hadn't an inch of shade to keep off the blistering sun. Rico backed unsteadily out of the trailer and stood with hanging head, his sides heaving and his neck all dark with sweat and grime. While Philippa held a pail of water for him, Mrs. Pappadou walked to the other side of the car so nobody would see her wipe her eyes. Mr. Pappadou looked very serious. He was thinking of how Philippa would feel if they could not save Rico.

Then suddenly Rico lifted his head. He pricked his ears and looked intently up the road. It was the first time for days he had shown a spark of interest in anything.

"Hey, what do you know!" exclaimed Mary Carey.

"What is it, Rico? What do you see?" asked Philippa, gently patting his neck. "Tell me!"

Rico, still looking West, gave a weak little whinny and the ghost of his old impatient head-toss.

"We must go on," said Mr. Pappadou.

The road was straight as a ruled line, but there were waves in it now. They would come up to a rise and look across a long dip to another rise they couldn't see over, a mile or so further on. In a little while, as they came to the top of one of these rises, Philippa suddenly shouted, "Look! Oh LOOK!"

Everybody looked. At first they couldn't see anything.

Then beyond the dull plain that stretched ahead, beyond the hard horizon they had grown so used to seeing, they made out something that hadn't been there before—a faint blue jagged line against the sky. Cloud, perhaps? Perhaps it wasn't even real.

"It is! It is!" cried Mary Carey and Philippa together. "It's the mountains!"

Seven

Late that afternoon they reached a big camping area near the town of Indian Springs in a wooded valley surrounded by peaks that were streaked with white. Snow! They were in the mountains!

The camping area was crowded, and as usual, children came running as soon as Rico was unloaded.

"I'm sorry but you'd better keep away. This pony has hippotoxicosis," said Mary Carey, "it might be catching."

Philippa and Mary Carey led Rico to a meadow bordered by a rushing blue-green stream that seemed in an awful hurry to get where it was going. The grass was thick with wild flowers. They watched with bated breath while Rico lowered his head. Would he eat? He nosed around in the grass, nibbled a flower here and there, and then to their heartfelt relief found a blue one with bell-shaped dangling blossoms that he munched greedily. For an hour he wandered in the meadow selecting the spikes of this blue flower. Then he picked his way to the edge of the creek for a long drink of the icy water.

"I think he looks better already," said Philippa as they led him back to camp.

They stayed two days at this campsite, and most of the time one of them was out in the meadow with Rico, standing guard against the children—and the grown-ups, too—who came to look at him and ask, *Why* does that pony wear a blanket?

Rico did seem to be happier. When he wasn't grazing on the blue flowers, he stood with pricked ears looking up at the mountains. He would even move his wings a little under the blanket. They were careful to take the blanket off as soon as it grew dark so he could shake and stretch, but all day long there were too many people around to take any chances.

"Be careful," warned Mr. Pappadou, "because if anyone suspects what kind of a horse Rico really is, the publicity would be terrible. Newspaper reporters would come from everywhere—cameras, movies, interviews—there'd be no peace. Rico would never get well. Can't you get rid of those children, Philippa?"

"I do," said Philippa. "I tell them he has hippo-whatever-it-is and they go away, but then new ones come."

"I wonder if that is a good idea," said Mr. Pappadou.

It turned out not to be a good idea. The Ranger arrived on the afternoon of the second day and told them they would have to leave.

"He hasn't really got hippotoxicosis," explained Mr. Pappadou. "We just said so because the children bothered us."

"Well, I don't know what he's got," said the Ranger, "but you'll have to take him away from here. It's against regulations, anyhow. Of course he's only a pony, and I might have overlooked the whole thing, but I've had complaints that there's a health hazard here. To tell the truth, I never seen a horse blanketed in this weather, and all swoll up under the blanket, too. He's not the right shape. There sure must be something wrong with him. I'm sorry, Mister, but you can't keep that horse here."

"We'll have to move again," said Mr. Pappadou. "It's too crowded here anyway. Mary Carey, you help Mama start packing and I'll go and make some inquiries."

"Oh dear," sighed Mrs. Pappadou, "I do hate to leave this beautiful spot."

"Maybe we'll find another just as good," said Mary Carey hopefully, "with no people."

Mr. Pappadou explained what he wanted to the man at the Tourist Information Booth at Indian Springs.

"You aren't going to find a camp where there are *no* other people," said the man, "unless you leave your car. Any of the outfitters in town could take your party up into the mountains with a packtrain, sir—across Elk

Creek to the Clearwater Range, or back into the Myths. There's a lot of places they could set you up in a nice quiet camp where you wouldn't see nobody."

"Outfitters?" said Mr. Pappadou. "Packtrain?"

"Yessir. A man who'll outfit you with saddle horses and pack animals to carry your stuff, and a dependable guide and a cook, too, if you need one."

"Well, my wife can cook," said Mr. Pappadou, "but she's never been on a horse, and she's rather nervous."

"That's too bad, but I'm afraid it's the only way she can get into the high country away from other people," said the man. "Unless of course, she wants to *walk*." He said this as if he'd heard of such a thing, but couldn't believe that anyone in their right mind would ever actually do it.

"Ride a horse!" exclaimed Mrs. Pappadou, when Mr. Pappadou told her what the man had said. "Me, Papa?" But when she heard that there just wasn't any other way to get Rico off to a lonely place where he could get strong and well, Mrs. Pappadou bravely agreed to try to ride a horse.

So Mr. Pappadou went to an outfitter and made arrangements. Philippa and Mary Carey whooped with joy at the idea of going camping on horseback with a train of packhorses. Mr. Pappadou took them into town to buy riding boots and blue jeans and cowboy hats, and, of course, warm shirts and jackets, because it's cold up high near the snow.

There was only one worry—would Rico be strong enough to make the trip?

"We'll tell the man to go very slowly, won't we, Papa?" Philippa asked anxiously.

"We certainly will!" said Mrs. Pappadou. "Me on a horse! Whoever would have imagined such a thing?"

"Don't be nervous, Mama," soothed Mr. Pappadou.

"You'll be all right on the horse you get from me, Ma'am," said Mr. Simpson, the outfitter. "I've got an old blue roan named Old Blue who'll take real good care of you."

"Oh dear, I hope so!" wailed Mrs. Pappadou.

Mr. Simpson looked puzzled when he heard that they had a horse of their own they wanted to take along on this trip even though no one was going to ride it. He offered to board it for them while they were away, but when they insisted that Rico *had* to go along, he simply shrugged his shoulders like a man who is used to the peculiar notions of dudes.

"Jim Randell will guide you," he said. "Jim's a good man, one of my best. But since you folks are in such a hurry to get going, I'll have to rustle up a packer for you around town here. None of my other regular boys is in just now. Well, I guess everything is settled then. You'll have your duffle and the extra horse at my place first thing in the morning. O.K.?"

"Yes, we will be very prompt," said Mr. Pappadou. "There is just one other thing, though, Mr. Simpson. Will you please tell your men not to ask any questions about our horse. He wears a blanket, and he does not look well. But we do not wish for any comments or advice about him, please. Will you tell your men that?"

"Why sure," said Mr. Simpson, "I'll tell them." He didn't seem surprised. Westerners do not like to seem surprised.

"I feel as if I was in fancy dress," said Mr. Pappadou the next morning, when he had put on his new Western clothes.

"You look very handsome, Papa," said Mrs. Pappadou.

But the truth is that Mr. Pappadou didn't really look as if he belonged in a big ten-gallon hat and high-heeled boots. His jeans seemed a little tight in the wrong places, and everything he had on was so very new.

Mrs. Pappadou didn't look Western—she just looked different. She had a straw hat tied under her chin with a bandanna because she said the cowgirl kind of hat gave her a headache, and she wore her own blouse and shoes and jacket because they were more comfortable. Her blue jeans were the only new things she had on.

"I do not think the good Lord designed me to wear pants," said Mrs. Pappadou.

Mary Carey and Philippa were so happy in their bright new shirts and jeans, and especially their big hats and high-heeled boots, that they were sure they looked wonderful. And they really did look very nice.

"Golly, Phil, I never thought Out West would really be all this Western!" remarked Mary Carey as she and Philippa sat on the top bar of the corral at Mr. Simpson's place and watched tents and duffle bags and bedrolls and boxes and boxes of food being loaded onto five packhorses and a white mule. The saddle horses which were to carry them into the mountains stood ready saddled in a line along a hitching rail. They stood with heads low, ears drooping, one hind leg bent, looking bored. One of them, a brown and white pinto, wore Philippa's saddle, the one Mr. Olympio had sent her for Rico.

When the last pack had been covered neatly with a tarp, and the ropes pulled tight, it was time to take Rico out of the trailer, which was parked nearby. He looked small and sick compared to Mr. Simpson's sleek horses. Philippa held Rico by his gold halter and patted his neck.

"Cheer up, Rico," she whispered. "We're going up where the snow is, near the sky!" As if he understood, Rico lifted his head, pricked his ears, and looked toward the mountains.

"Well," said Mr. Simpson, "I guess we're all set. This is Jim Randell, folks. He's your guide. Jim knows these mountains like the back of his hand—born and raised in 'em. You won't have one thing to worry about with Jim in charge!"

The younger of the two men who had been packing the horses stepped up and shook hands with Mr. and Mrs. Pappadou. Then he winked at Philippa and gave Mary Carey a nod and a smile. He had blue eyes and a brown face and the most beautiful curl to the brim of his hat. Philippa liked him right away.

The other man didn't smile and didn't come to shake hands. He had narrow eyes that didn't seem to look in the same direction.

"This is Jake Turpin," said Mr. Simpson. "He's going along as packer." Jake grunted without looking up from

coiling a rope. Philippa wondered why he looked so cross.

The moment had come for them to mount their horses—the moment Mrs. Pappadou had been dreading ever since they decided to go on a pack trip.

After he had tightened all the girths, Jim untied a speckled gray mare from the rail and led her over to a sort of platform. Mrs. Pappadou could step right off this mounting block into the saddle.

"Well, thank goodness," she said. "I never could have got up from the ground."

Jim adjusted the stirrups so they were comfortable and showed her how to hold the reins.

"You just leave everything to Old Blue, Ma'am," he said. "She knows all there is to know about her business, so don't worry. Leave the reins nice and loose, like so."

"She won't run away or do anything sudden?" asked Mrs. Pappadou nervously.

"Not her!" Jim reassured her. He took Old Blue by the rein and led her a few steps. Mrs. Pappadou grabbed the pommel, looking scared, but when nothing happened she smiled shakily.

"Me on a horse!" she said. She even sounded a little bit proud.

"Once you get the hang of it, Ma'am," said Jim, "you're going to like it just fine."

Mr. Pappadou's horse was named Freddy—a big bay with a white blaze down his nose. Mary Carey's was a sorrel mare ("to match my complexion," said Mary Carey) named Chiquita. Philippa's brown and white pinto had one blue eye.

"He's got a watch eye," said Jim. "Makes him look spooky—like he's mean or skittish, but it don't mean a thing. He's steady as they make 'em."

"What's his name?" asked Philippa, who thought he looked lovely.

"Three Cheers," said Jim, giving her a leg up.

"Three Cheers?"

"Hip, hip, hooray!" cried Mary Carey.

They were all ready to go.

Philippa wanted to lead Rico herself, but it was decided it would be better if Jim led him, and Philippa rode right behind to keep an eye on him and see how he was doing.

Jim tied one end of a long rope to Rico's halter and led him over to where his own horse stood waiting. Rico looked poor and gaunt beside the glossy little mare.

Jim's mare, whose name was Cindy, gave a startled snort when she saw Rico, but after she'd stretched out her neck and they'd touched noses, they seemed to be friends. Jim mounted and moved away and Rico followed obediently behind. The other horses fell into line—Jake, yelling and chasing the packhorses, brought up the rear.

They were off.

"Don't go too fast, please," begged Mrs. Pappadou. "You won't gallop or anything?" Jim said no, a good steady walk was the way to travel on the trail.

To begin with, Philippa had to get used to Three Cheers—riding him was so different from riding Rico. But Jim gave her pointers, and soon she felt quite at home and could look around and talk and ask questions without thinking about what she was doing.

Jim wasn't a bit hard to talk to. The more she talked to him, the nicer he seemed to her to be. Why, she thought suddenly, wasn't he just exactly what Mary Carey and she were looking for? There was just one thing . . .

"Jim," said Philippa, "do you have a ranch?"

"Well, that's a painful subject with me right now," said Jim. "The answer is, no I haven't, and present prospects are I won't never have one."

"Oh dear!" cried Philippa. "Oh dear! I'm so sorry!"

"Well, thanks for the sympathy," said Jim. "How come you asked?"

"I just thought you might," said Philippa. She felt discouraged. She began to be afraid they wouldn't ever find a cowboy with a ranch for Mary Carey to marry.

By noon they had climbed out of the valley. They ate lunch beside a little creek that tumbled across the trail. Looking out through the trunks of pine trees they could see across the valley a row of pinky-tan peaks streaked with snow. The sun was hot, but in the shade a brisk little breeze had an edge to it.

"Ouch!" said Mrs. Pappadou, as Jim helped her off Old Blue.

"I feel stiff too, Mama," said Mr. Pappadou, "but look at the flowers!"

There were lots of flowers, many of them new ones, growing along the creek banks, and the grass under the pines was full of them. Rico sniffed at them and then quickly began to graze, moving eagerly from one clump to another. Mary Carey nudged Philippa.

"Look at that!" she whispered. "If he keeps that up, kid, we've won!"

After a rest they went on again. Philippa rode behind Jim as before.

"My goodness, Philippa!" said Mrs. Pappadou after a while. "You will make Jim quite exhausted with your questions."

"Don't worry about me, Ma'am," laughed Jim, turning in his saddle to look back at Mrs. Pappadou. "We've been talking about horses. That's a long-winded subject."

Before they reached camp that afternoon, Philippa had found out about every horse Jim had ever known, and a good deal about cattle, sheep, bears, mountain lions, pack rats, side-hill gougers, rodeos, roundups, and other Western subjects. Jim sat sideways in his saddle and answered all her questions, but though he looked at Rico from time to time in a puzzled way, he didn't ask any questions himself.

When people talk about horses, they like to talk about

their horse — if they are lucky enough to have one — and Philippa was dying to tell Jim all about Rico. But she didn't. All she said was, "He came from across the sea. He belongs to a special breed that's very *very* rare."

"Seems sure-footed," Jim remarked, cautiously.

"Well, he ought to be," said Philippa. "Cliffs and precipices are what he's used to. He likes them. That's why we brought him to the mountains."

Jim looked at Rico again, climbing steadily up the rough trail behind Cindy. The thin strands of his golden halter gleamed in the sun. He was sweating under the blanket that covered his back. Jim didn't say anything.

"Jim, what's your favorite color of a horse?" asked Philippa. Jim said it was the color of the best horse he could lay his hands on at the moment.

"At the present time it's Cindy, this mare I'm riding now," he said.

"She's pretty!" admired Philippa. "She's a buckskin, isn't she?"

"A golden buckskin," said Jim.

"I like her black trimmings." Cindy had a black stripe down the middle of her back, and a glossy black mane and tail that set off the golden color of her sleek coat.

"She's clever and easy gaited and tough as nails besides — the smartest cow-horse I ever rode," Jim went on. "That's partly my own pride, of course, because I raised her and broke her myself."

"You did?" cried Philippa. "You raised her from a foal?"

"Yes, and pretty soon I'm going to breed her and see if I can raise another as good as she is."

"Who'll be the father?" asked Philippa.

"I was thinking of a stallion of Mr. Simpson's called Black Magic. He's a good stud. Mr. Simpson's raised some nice foals by him."

"Oh," cried Philippa, "I've never seen a newborn foal! Someday—" she began, and looked back over her shoulder to where Mary Carey rode at the end of the line. "Someday, when Mary Carey gets her ranch . . ."

"That young lady back there? Is she interested in a ranch?"

"Oh, yes," cried Philippa. "She's terribly interested. She's going to raise horses on her ranch, and I can choose any one I want for my very own."

"Now won't that be nice?" said Jim. "Where is this ranch going to be at?"

"Well, we don't know yet, exactly," said Philippa. "It depends."

"My Dad has a ranch she might buy, if . . ." Jim's voice trailed off as if he didn't really believe what he was saying.

"Oh she can't *buy* a ranch!" exclaimed Philippa. "She hasn't enough money for that. The only thing she can do is marry a cowboy who already has one."

Jim looked startled.

"I see what you mean—it depends," he said.

"If your Dad has a ranch," said Philippa after a pause, "why can't you have part of it?"

"The reasons," said Jim, "are too many to go into. What they all add up to is dollars."

"What a shame!" Philippa sighed. For a while she

didn't say anything. Then suddenly she asked another question: "Jim, are you married?"

"Who, me?" Jim squinted up his blue eyes and took a long look at Philippa. Then he glanced back down the line of riders.

"Sure," he said. He drew off his left glove and held up his hand to show a broad gold ring, glinting on his fourth finger. "I sure am."

"Oh dear," sighed Philippa again. After a long time she asked Jim what his wife's name was.

"Her name? Name is Sadie," said Jim.

"Is she a cowgirl?"

"Bet your life," said Jim. "Like it says in the song:

She's wild and woolly and full of fleas
And hard to curry below the knees.

Six-shooter Sadie, the She-wolf from Sour Creek, they used to call her. That was before we was married, of course. She's tamed down some since, but she's still mighty quick on the draw. Goes in for bronc riding in the rodeo—in the money, too. Whenever she wants a new horse, she goes out and catches her a wild mustang, breaks him in, and rides him . . ." Jim kept thinking of more things to tell Philippa about Sadie, who seemed to be a very outstanding kind of cowgirl. Some of the things she could do sounded almost—well, hard to believe. But Philippa didn't feel any enthusiasm for her. She didn't even want to meet her—in fact, she only wished Sadie had never been born.

Eight

The last stretch of trail before they reached Camas Creek, the place where they were going to camp for their first night, climbed in short zigzags up a really steep slope. Mrs. Pappadou hung onto the pommel with both hands, looking steadily up because she didn't dare look down. Mr. Pappadou, who had been complaining because he couldn't stop to look at the interesting flowers he saw, could pick flowers now on the uphill side as he rode by. Mary Carey, who did dare to look down, was fascinated to watch the packhorses, like fat gray bundles with heads and tails, creeping slowly and jerkily up the zigzags far below.

But Philippa didn't look at the scenery or the flowers. Rico was limping!

"Jim," she cried in distress, "something is wrong with Rico! Look how he walks."

"I know. He's been favoring that off forefoot for quite a spell." Jim turned and watched Rico's head moving up and down and his uneven gait. "I didn't want to say anything, but I had a hunch the going would be rough for him, soft as he is, without any shoes, so I threw a set of small shoes in the pack, just in case. We'll tack 'em on him before we start in the morning, and he'll be O.K."

Philippa felt relieved.

Fortunately, they didn't have much further to go. They soon reached the top of a rise where the trail leveled off in a meadow bordered by open pine woods and bright with wildflowers. Through the center of the meadow, bushy willows marked the course of a little creek.

"Well, here we are, folks, Camas Creek," announced Jim, dismounting in a trampled spot near the charred remains of a fire. There were no other people there, but there were plenty of signs that people had been there—papers and cans and bottles and other messy things all scattered around.

"Now, Philippa, you take charge of your pony here. That's right, just let Three Cheers go—I'll tend to him."

While the men were tying up the packhorses, beginning to unpack them and to set up camp, Philippa and Mary Cary led Rico out along the creek until the willows hid them from view.

"Phil, what in the world was all that you were saying to Jim?" asked Mary Carey.

"I didn't say anything," said Philippa.

"Well, you sure did a lot of talking for somebody who wasn't saying anything."

"He's got a ranch," said Philippa, "or at least his Dad has, only Jim can't ever have it because it's got to be sold, and anyhow he's married already to a cowgirl named Sadie. It's just a big shame—and he raises horses, too. That beautiful mare he's riding, her name is Cindy. Someday she's going to have a foal."

"And surely, you found out what his grandmother's first name was?"

"No, why? Oh dear, it's just too bad, Mary Carey," Philippa went on. "You'll have to find some other cowboy to marry, only I don't think there is one as nice as Jim. I don't like Jake Turpin, do you? His eyes look in different directions, and he yells at the packhorses and hits them with the end of his rope. I think he's mean."

"Phil, dear, suppose we drop the whole subject," said Mary Carey. "What we've got to do now is get Rico built up. That's what we came for and that's what we're going to concentrate on. So you let me do my own marrying in my own good time, O.K.? Here. I think it's safe to take the blanket off here. Whoa, Rico."

Rico gave a tremendous shake as soon as the blanket was off. Then he lifted his wings and stretched them the way a person stretches his arms. Then he flapped them, shook them again, folded them into place, and with a contented look around at the snow peaks, he started cropping the flowers that starred the grass. He still looked thin and poor, but even after the tiring climb his spirits were good.

"Rico, old boy, you're a different person from what you were three days ago," said Mary Carey, patting his neck. Philippa gave him a big happy hug.

Blue smoke presently began to rise from among the pines. By the time the girls led Rico back to camp, the saddles and pack saddles were stacked on the ground, and the horses, dark wet patches showing where they had sweated under their saddlepads, were already hobbled and contentedly grazing, or rolling to scratch their itchy backs. A fire was blazing and Jim and Jake were setting up the tents. What had lately been just an untidy piece of outdoors suddenly looked like home.

Mrs. Pappadou was busy picking up cans and bottles and papers to make things neater.

"I thought if I bent some different muscles it might make the riding muscles less stiff," she said ruefully. "Oh dear, I just don't understand how people can be so messy!"

Mr. Pappadou was carrying the duffles and sleeping bags over to the tents.

Before long they were sitting down to supper around a cheerful fire. A row of mountains across the valley shone bright pink in the sunset glow, while the peaks on their side towered dark and cold against an orange sky.

"Boy," exclaimed Mary Carey happily, "this is *camping!* Sure different from what we've been doing!"

"No motor noises and smells," said Mrs. Pappadou.

"Nobody's picked all the flowers," said Mr. Pappadou.

"What I like about it here is no other people," began Philippa. She didn't get any further because just at that moment a voice said—"Hi!"—and two people walked into the firelight out of the dusk.

They were a young man with a beard and a young woman with long straight yellow hair. They had on heavy boots and carried big packs, which they eased onto the ground as if they were glad to put them down. Each had a sort of pickaxe in his hand, and the young man carried a big coil of rope.

"Hello," he said. "I'm Tony Hartshorne, and this is my wife Lisa. We'd have got here before dark, only we had trouble crossing Myth Creek. Do you mind if we cook our supper over your fire?"

"Oh, please, please sit down," said Mrs. Pappadou. "Haven't we some supper left, Jim?" Jim was already stirring up the coals under the coffee pot.

"Sure thing," he said. "Biscuits, beans, steak . . ."

"Steak!" cried the two Hartshornes together.

"Haven't you got any horses?" asked Philippa, when their plates had been filled and they were settled near the fire.

"Nope, backpacking," said Tony, his mouth full of steak. "The trouble with horses is—you know—grass. We've got to be free to go high and stay there. Horses limit your options. You know, you have to camp where the horses want to be, not where you do."

"I never thought of that," said Mary Carey. "But then you have to carry all your food and stuff yourselves."

"Sure," answered Tony, "so what? You give up steak, but look what you win. When you spend the night on a ledge halfway to the stars—you know—you don't kick

about the menu. Besides, whatever it is—soup, sausage, chocolate—it tastes better than a banquet. You don't envy anybody in the world."

"Gee!" said Mary Carey.

"And if you run out of grub—well, you can always eat the flowers."

"Eat the *flowers?*" cried Philippa.

"Oh, not all of them, of course," said Tony, "but some have starchy roots, or bulbs, or edible seeds, some make greens—you just have to take the trouble to find out. The settlers learned from the Indians, but—you know—it's in books now."

"That camas," said Jim, "the blue flower that's in bloom now, folks used to depend on the roots of that a lot in the early days. I know that for a fact. But I never ate any myself."

"We have," said Lisa.

"It gives you a feeling," said Tony. "Living off the land. I don't know what there is about it—satisfies something that goes way back, something primitive between people and—you know—nature."

"Just the same," said Lisa, "people shouldn't do it unless they absolutely have to or there won't be any wild flowers left."

"Rico seems to like the blue ones best," said Philippa. "But he doesn't eat enough to matter."

"This camping," remarked Mrs. Pappadou thoughtfully, "it is a strange thing. It is an idea, I think, and it seems to be a different idea for every person. Your idea" (she was talking to the Hartshornes) "is a beautiful one—to travel light, free, to go anywhere, carrying what you need on your own backs. Philippa and Mary Carey want adventure, and only with horses, I think. For me, camping is to be close to the beauty of nature, to live simply and quietly among birds and flowers and all the wonders of earth. What do you think about camping, Jim?"

"Well, Ma'am," said Jim, "personally, I think it's hard work. To tell the truth, I've often figured I wouldn't mind traveling around in one of those land yachts you see pictures of—the kind with hot water and good beds and lights and all—no tent poles to cut or wood to chop or water to lug. Sounds like a pretty good way to see the world."

"I agree with you, Jim," said Mr. Pappadou, "in a way, that is. When we were on our way out here, I saw quite a few of those units and I made up my mind I'd get one for my family, and one of the best. But I've sort of changed my idea. If you have all the same things when you are camping that you have when you are at home, why leave home? Camping—I think it suggests something simple, like what Mama says. Yes, I've changed my idea."

"You'd have trouble getting up here in a land yacht," remarked Tony Hartshorne.

"I've noticed," said Jim, "that the men I guide hunting and fishing, from cities mostly—they seem to set as much store by their week in camp as they do by the game they get. Breaking ice in the bucket, grub cooked on the fire—all that pioneer stuff seems to mean a lot to them."

"Of course," said Tony, "the poor guys' one chance to

get out from under—office, traffic jam, smog, TV . . ."

"What do you say, Mr. Turpin?" asked Mrs. Pappadou kindly, since no one had said a word to Jake all evening. "What is your idea of camping?"

"Bunk! No sense to it," growled Jake. "Anybody got a decent roof over his head and sets out to go camping when he don't got to, he's a fool or else he's crazy, one or t'other."

Jim laughed. "Strikes me you've got a case of the agins tonight, Jake," he said. But Jake didn't answer.

"Where did you two come from?" Mary Carey asked the Hartshornes.

"Myth Peak," they answered together.

They were mountain climbers. They'd been trying to climb the northeast ridge of Myth Peak—a much harder route than the one from Myth Valley on the west. They hadn't made it because of bad weather.

"But we'll have another try," said Tony, "after we've rested up and got some more grub."

"You mean you go up those cliffs, pounding nails into cracks, and hanging on by a rope—like real Alpine stuff?" asked Mary Carey, much interested.

"Pitons, not nails," said Tony. "We use climbing techniques, if that's what you mean."

"I guess that's what I mean," said Mary Carey. She turned and looked at the peaks behind them, dark purple now against a pale green sky. "Is that Myth Peak there? Gee, would I ever be thrilled to climb a mountain like that! But I guess that's one thing I'll never get a chance to take up."

"Well, it might be you can go to the top of Myth Peak without mountain-climbing techniques pretty soon," said Jim. "Haven't you heard about the Myth Valley development plan?"

"I've heard of it of course, but I just couldn't believe it," said Tony. "Myth Valley—the most beautiful, high, lonely, lovely spot—to blast a road in there and make it just like everywhere else—hotels, stores, crowds, land yachts, and worst of all, a lift to the top of the mountain! Somewhere else—anywhere else—but not Myth Valley, and not that peak! Is there a real chance the thing will go through?"

"The only thing stopping them now," said Jim, "is they don't have Lost Canyon. That's the one practical way in—the only place they could put a road in to the valley. It's not for sale, but they may have a way to force the owner to sell."

"Sure he'll sell," grumped Jake. "He's just holding out for more money. Money, that's what. Money'll buy Myth Valley or anything else. They ante up the right price, he'll sell. Gol-durned fool if he don't."

"Well, all I can say is . . ." began Jim, looking disgusted. But whatever it was he could say, he didn't say it. Instead, he got up and walked out into the dark for a log for the fire, and when he threw it on, sparks flew in all directions.

Philippa was beginning to feel sleepy, but there was one thing she wanted to know.

"Why do they call it Myth Valley? And Myth Peak, what does it mean?"

"I've heard," said Tony, "that an old prospector, who used to go off for months and years to live with the Indians, or maybe alone, with only wild animals for friends, got lost in a snow storm. He finally struggled down into a little hidden valley. Afterwards, when he got back to wherever he came from, he kept telling anybody who would listen about this valley—how it was the most beautiful place, and how it had everything—water, game, fish, the biggest timber and the brightest flowers—you know— the way he described it, it was an out-of-this-world kind of dream. Well, he was old and sick and he could never go back. And nobody else could find the place from his description. So they said he'd dreamed it—it was just a myth. Old So-and-so and his Myth Valley. Then, years later, some relation of his, somebody who remembered the story, found just such a valley and he figured it must be what the old man had been talking about. So he called it Myth Valley, and the big mountain that's to the east of it—that one up there—just sort of took the name, too—Myth Peak. The lower ones are Marvel and South Myth."

"Papa, can't we gooo-oooh-aaah-hoo to Myth Valley?" Philippa yawned so hard nobody could understand what she said.

"Bed," said Mary Carey. "Come on, kid. We'll check on Rico, and then we'll hit the hay."

Rico was just fine.

Nine

Next morning, loud clanging bells and the thumping of hobbled horses woke Mary Carey and Philippa in their tent, and a wonderful smell of woodsmoke and bacon helped them out of their sleeping bags and into their cold clothes.

Philippa hurried through her breakfast, leaving Mary Carey to wash up while she led Rico out of sight of camp to graze and stretch his wings. He flapped them so hard when she took off the blanket that he lifted all four feet off the ground. Then he began feeding as if he were starved. Almost all the flowers he found seemed to appeal to him.

By the time Rico was satisfied and Philippa had led him back, the horses were saddled and the packhorses were being loaded. Before long the cozy camp had turned back into scenery again—and thanks to Mrs. Pappadou's efforts, it was cleaner and more attractive scenery than they had found it.

But before they started, Rico had to be shod.

"Not the best job in the world," Jim said when he had finished, "but if they stay on until we get to the Meadows, that'll be long enough."

"Lousy job," grunted Jake Turpin, who had stood watching. "Doggone pony all wropped up like a sick cat. No sense to it!"

He spat on the ground. Then, as he walked scowling past Rico, Rico did something he had never done before—never. He jerked up his head, laid his ears flat back, lunged forward, and gave Jake a good sharp nip in the arm.

"You ding-blasted sneaky little . . ." Jake swung the bridle he was holding and would have hit Rico over the head with it, bit and all, except that Rico wheeled away too fast for him.

Jim spoke sharply to Jake and got things calmed down, but everybody felt very uncomfortable.

"Such language!" Mrs. Pappadou murmured to Mr. Pappadou. "So ugly in this beautiful place."

Mary Carey gave Philippa a warning look. "We've got to watch that Jake," she whispered. "There's something wrong with that guy—and Rico knows it, too. He could be dangerous."

Of course the Hartshornes had been up and packed and away long before the Pappadou party were ready.

Tony and Lisa had said thank you for the steak, and waved a cheerful good-bye as they swung off down the trail. Mary Carey looked enviously after them.

"It must be great," she said, "just picking up and going where you feel like—on the loose like that."

"I wouldn't want to camp without horses," said Philippa.

Now, at last, they were ready to start, too.

"Where are we going today, Jim?" asked Mr. Pappadou. "I was wondering—if it would be possible—this Myth Valley they were talking about, is that far from here? That young man said the flowers are especially fine there."

"Yessir, they are. I guided a man in there last summer—he was a botany professor, and he said there wasn't another place in the whole of the mountains could touch Myth Valley for flowers. That's what he said."

Mr. Pappadou began to look very excited. Philippa bounced up and down in her saddle, startling Three Cheers, who looked as if he might begin to bounce too. Philippa stopped.

"Oh Jim! Myth Valley. Please, let's go to Myth Valley!" All those wonderful flowers, she thought to herself, would be just the thing for Rico.

But Jim shook his head.

"Myth Valley is a hard place to get to from anywhere," he said, "but it's about impossible from this side. See that ridge?" He pointed to a shoulder of the peak above them. "The only way into the valley from this side is over a saddle back of that hump there—you can't see the place from here. That's Black Saturday Pass. It's a really tough, rough climb—you can't call it a trail. What I mean, it's *steep*. Falling rocks, too—and blocked with snow as often as not. The last time I tried it I had to turn around and come back down. It was no go—not even for Cindy, who's the best mountain climber of a horse I've ever seen."

"Oh my gracious, oh please, don't even talk about it!" cried Mrs. Pappadou.

"What I figured to do if you folks agree," said Jim, "was to go up here to the Myth Meadows. That's on this side of the mountain, right under the cliffs. There's a good place to camp, hardly anybody goes there much. You'd be—you know—off by yourselves. There's flowers there too, sure to be, if that's what you're looking for."

"That sounds much better," said Mrs. Pappadou, relieved.

"We'll have to ford Myth Creek to get there," said Jim, "but that's not near as bad as it looks."

Soon they were on the trail again.

They decided to let Rico travel between Mary Carey and Philippa without being led. It worked well—he gave no trouble beyond a pause now and then to snatch a clump of flowers from the edge of the trail. The shoes seemed to help him, for he no longer limped.

He gave no trouble, that is, until afternoon, when they were all tired and anxious to reach their camping place, which Jim said was only a short way further on. They had crossed a pass and plunged down into a valley, out of which they were climbing again now. Suddenly the trail disappeared into a wide creek that roared and crashed down its bed of boulders. Jim's mare plunged in and picked her way across; milky green water piled up against her legs and splashed Jim's boots and chaps.

Philippa was scared. But Jim shouted to her above the roar to let Three Cheers come, to give him his head and let him come. Slowly, bumpily, Three Cheers felt for his footing, his hoofs making a hollow, watery clunk on the slippery boulders. Philippa held on to the pommel like grim death and tried not to look at the dizzy rush of water that nearly touched her stirrups. What a relief when they scrambled safely up the bank on the other side.

It was Rico's turn next. Lowering his head, he took one horrified look at the jumble of rocks and foam, and then with an outraged snort, backed up with a bump into Mary Carey on Chiquita.

"Whoa, Rico!" said Mary Carey. "Steady, boy!"

Mrs. Pappadou, who was behind Mary Carey, and who was nervous already about crossing the creek, got even more nervous.

"Oh dear! Old Blue! What shall we do? What shall we do?" she moaned, and pulled too hard on the reins, which is what inexperienced riders do when they are nervous. Old Blue backed up obediently, bump into Mr. Pappadou's Freddy.

"Here come the packhorses," said Mr. Pappadou. "Dear me!"

"Hey, keep a-moving! What in tarnation's wrong up there!" yelled Jake from the end of the line. Altogether it was quite a traffic jam.

Mary Carey got off Chiquita and took Rico by the halter.

"Come on, boy," she said soothingly, leading him forward to the water. He went apprehensively, ears forward, eyes rolling. At the edge he stopped again, snorting and frightened. Philippa called him from the other side, but Rico wouldn't budge.

"Now what!" thought Mary Carey.

At this moment, Jake's horse came pushing around the line of riders through the brush.

"What's up?" called Jake in his rasping voice. "Oh—so Mama's pet don't want to get his feet wet, hey? Well, I reckon we'll have to persuade him!" Before Mary Carey knew what he was up to, Jake swung the loose end of his rope and brought it down with a wicked whack on Rico's rump.

Rico was outraged. Rearing and plunging he broke away from Mary Carey and crashed into the thick underbrush in a panic.

Jake dismounted. His face was red and he wore an ugly smile.

"I'll show that little . . ."

"You leave him alone," cried Mary Carey, blocking the way. "Don't you dare touch Rico!"

"You shut up!" growled Jake, and started to push past her.

"Oh no you don't!" cried Mary Carey.

What happened next happened so fast that it was all over before any of them understood what was going on, even though all of them were watching—Mr. and Mrs. Pappadou from one side of the creek, Philippa from the other, and Jim from halfway across, as he made his way back to see what was the matter. All they saw was that at one moment, Jake stood angrily trying to push Mary Carey aside so he could get to Rico, and the next he windmilled gracefully through the air and landed with a splash, flat on his back in the creek.

Jim reined in his horse in midstream and sat in utter amazement while Jake heaved himself to his feet, cursing and dripping, mounted his horse, and rode back in savage silence to his place behind the packtrain.

Then Jim began to laugh. He laughed so hard that he couldn't speak. He came ashore laughing and got off his horse, but he was laughing so hard he couldn't stand up. He sat down on a boulder, rocking helplessly back and forth, and looked at Mary Carey.

"Wha . . . what . . . ?" But he couldn't get it out. He was helpless.

"That big ox," he gasped. "Just a girl . . . oh, Mary Carey! . . . Holy nightshirt! Never, no, I never seen the beat . . . Never, never, never . . . !"

"It's not all that hard when you know how," said Mary Carey, modestly.

"But the way you swung him right over your head into that creek! Talk about bull-dogging! Mary Carey, you're

". . . you're . . ." Jim didn't have breath enough to finish.

"It's just judo," said Mary Carey. "I'm not really so hot. I only took it up a couple of years ago."

"Jim! Mary Carey!" came a wail from Mrs. Pappadou. "Please, what are we going to do?" Philippa on the other side of the creek was shouting, too.

"It's O.K., Phil," Mary Carey called back. "We're coming. Don't worry."

"Listen, Jim," she went on. "You get Mr. and Mrs. Pappadou across, and the packtrain, and leave me here. Phil and I'll bring Rico. Just go on—get everybody across and keep going. Especially our wet friend. Don't let him come back, for goodness' sake!"

Jim didn't want to. He said it wasn't right to leave one of his dudes to cross that creek alone, even a super-duper dude like Mary Carey. But Mary Carey insisted there was no other way.

"Just tell Philippa to stay over there and call Rico as loud as she can when I give her the signal. And tie Chiquita here, please, so she won't follow you. Now go on."

Mary Carey ran to the Pappadous and whispered something to them. Then she went to catch Rico. She stood holding him by his halter, talking to him and stroking his neck, while the packtrain, with Jake glumly urging them on, forded the creek. Jim rode close behind Mrs. Pappadou as Old Blue felt her way cautiously across.

"I just shut my eyes and hung on," Mrs. Pappadou said afterward. "If I was ever more frightened in my life I don't know when it was."

Finally they had all crossed and disappeared around a bend in the trail. Chiquita, whom Jim had tied to a tree, looked after them anxiously, whinnying and pawing the ground. Philippa, on the other side of the creek, seemed to be having trouble with Three Cheers, too. Even the quietest horses don't like to be left behind.

Mary Carey waved to Philippa.

"Ready," she shouted. She unbuckled the blanket and pulled it off Rico's back.

"Rico! Come! Come, Rico, come, come, come!" Philippa's voice sounded small and shrill over the roar of the water.

Rico pricked his ears and looked toward her. Then he bent his head and sniffed at the foamy water's edge, blowing through wide nostrils. Suddenly he backed up as before, but purposefully this time, not in panic. Then with a rattle and a whoosh, he spread his wings and sprang out over the turbulent water, and in less than half a second he landed on the other side.

Three Cheers shied so violently when Rico swooped down beside him that Philippa fell off. Fortunately she had the presence of mind to keep fast hold of the reins, so he didn't get away.

Mary Carey hurriedly bundled up the blanket onto her saddle, untied the impatient Chiquita, mounted, and splashed across.

"Are you all in a piece, kid?" she asked anxiously. Philippa had her arms around Rico's neck, laughing and hugging him.

"Of course," she said. "Oh, isn't Rico wonderful, Mary Carey!"

They blanketed him again, and soon joined the others who were waiting for them around a bend in the trail. Jake wasn't with them—he had gone ahead with the packtrain.

Jim gave Rico a sharp look as he came along, bundled up in his blanket as usual. Then he turned an astonished, incredulous eye on Mary Carey. Mary Carey wondered why—and then suddenly she understood. The other horses were all wet from the ford, tails dripping, bellies splashed, legs soaked and shining. There wasn't a wet hair on Rico.

"Maybe he thinks I threw him across by judo," reflected Mary Carey. "From the way he's looking at me, he must think I did it."

Jim didn't say anything. In fact, he hardly said another word until they caught up with the packhorses in a high meadow that opened out before them at the top of a long hard climb through the spruce forest.

Ten

This time there was no trampled grass; there were no cans and papers to show that people had been there before. The bare cliffs of a magnificent peak walled in the long narrow park on one side. On the other it looked across a deep valley to a row of snow mountains with other snow mountains behind them and still others behind those, row after row, growing bluer and hazier until they met the hazy blue horizon a hundred miles away.

"Oh!" cried Mrs. Pappadou. "Oh!" She couldn't say another word. But Mr. Pappadou didn't see the mountains. "Look at the flowers!" he almost shouted. "Look at the FLOWERS!" The ground was so thickly covered with mats of blue and white and pink and yellow and purple flowers that there was scarcely room for grass. None of them grew more than a few inches high—indeed there were mats of tiny forget-me-nots and pinks that weren't even an inch. Mr. Pappadou was off his horse in an instant and kneeling among them as if each tiny mound was made of precious stones.

"Yes, the flowers, too," agreed Mrs. Pappadou. "Papa, I have to say it was worth being so frightened to see this place. Worth being so—oh dear!—so stiff and sore, also," she went on, dismounting rather painfully. "It is not your fault, Old Blue. You are a very kind horse. And you are much braver than I am, though that is not much of a compliment." She patted Old Blue's shoulder, darker gray now with sweat from the climb.

Jim found a circle of stunted firs that provided shelter from the wind and was handy to water. Here he and Jake, still scowling and sulky, set up the tents and picked a spot for the cook fire.

"Mary Carey, suppose you and I try making the biscuits," said Mrs. Pappadou. "We will take over the kitchen from Jim."

"O.K." said Mary Carey. "Boy, what a kitchen," she added, looking around. "But you know me when it comes to meals—I'm pretty good with a can opener."

Philippa, in the meantime, led Rico away from camp behind some trees to graze on the flowers.

Rico was a completely different horse. He dragged Philippa eagerly from one clump of tiny plants to another, cropping off the blossoms with a crisp, tearing sound, followed by a contented crunch, crunch, crunch of his grinding teeth. He seemed to like especially the little mats of blue forget-me-nots. The more he ate, the livelier he grew. He would raise his head, prick his ears, and look intently at the mountains in one direction, then ruffling his wings and shifting his feet in a frisky little prance, he'd turn and stand, head high and alert, looking the other way. Then he'd briskly go back to grazing, almost pulling the lead-rope out of Philippa's hand with eager tugs of his head. All the time as he grazed he kept raising and ruffling his wings.

"He wants to fly," thought Philippa. Joy and relief filled her heart. Rico was getting well.

"Pretty good biscuits for a jiujitsu expert," said Jim at supper.

"Heck, I was just looking on this time," said Mary Carey. "Tomorrow will be the test. Hope your teeth are all sharpened up."

"I've got a real good axe," said Jim.

Philippa took Rico out again before bedtime, and Mary Carey went with her.

It seemed dark and cold at first, but once away from the fire, they found they could see quite clearly. Millions upon millions of stars glittered above them, lighting Myth Peak, and even the faraway summits, with an eerie glow. Such a sky! It was as if they had been looking at the stars through a dirty windowpane all their lives, and now for the first time the window had been thrown open. The starlight seemed to go to Rico's head; he pranced and pulled at the lead-rope as if the minute he was rid of the blanket he would spread his wings and soar off into the spangled sky.

"Haven't we gone far enough?" asked Philippa. "They can't see us here."

"Just a bit further," said Mary Carey. "Behind that clump there."

They led Rico to the other side of a shadowy group of spruces. Not even a glint of the campfire was visible from here.

"This should be safe," said Mary Carey. "Whoa, Rico. Stand still while I take the blanket off. Whoa! Stand still, boy. What's the matter with you?"

Rico was fidgeting, ears up, staring into the dark.

"He sees something," said Philippa.

"Or hears something," said Mary Carey. "Wait a minute, what was that?"

Rico snorted.

"Oh dear, suppose it's a mountain lion . . ." began Philippa with a shiver. "Jim says they won't attack you unless they're wounded or cornered. Suppose he thinks we're trying to corner him?"

"Then he'd be pretty dumb—he's got all outdoors. But a bear?"

"A grizzly! Jim says you never know what they'll do. Oh Mary Carey, I'm scared."

Just then whatever it was sneezed—a loud, explosive sneeze, unmistakably human. It came from behind the spruce clump.

"I'll bet it's Jake," whispered Mary Carey. "That creep."

"Oh dear! He wants revenge because you threw him in

the creek. He's probably armed to the teeth. What shall we do?"

"Nonsense, what he wants is to find out about Rico. He's been dying of curiosity right from the start. Shhh, pretend you didn't hear anything . . . Well, Rico," Mary Carey said in a loud voice, "if you aren't going to eat, we may as well go back to camp. Come on, Phil."

They walked back, making a big circle around the spruce clump. Rico was jumpy and nervous, and Philippa had shivers between her shoulder blades all the way. But nothing happened.

When they reached the comfortable circle of firelight, Jake wasn't anywhere around. But then they didn't expect he would be.

They tied Rico to a tree near the tent and went to bed.

The next morning Jim asked Mr. Pappadou if they were satisfied with this as their permanent camp.

"I don't think people'll bother you up here. It's a kind of a dead end—no way out except Black Saturday Pass, of course. But like I told you, hardly anybody wants to risk that. Most of the trips go down Myth Creek to the Forks and out over Skyward Pass, or follow Clearwater Creek into the Watapoosie country."

"Oh, this is perfect. It is just right, Jim. I can't imagine that the flowers are any better even in Myth Valley," said Mr. Pappadou. "I am going to see how many I can collect and identify—I shall be very busy."

"And I am going to look at the view," said Mrs. Pappadou. "If I had come here in an automobile, I would say this is a beautiful view. But since I worked so hard to get here and was so frightened and uncomfortable, I say this is *my* view. I've earned it, and it's the most beautiful view in the world. I'm going to sit and enjoy it."

"Well, that's good, Ma'am," said Jim. "Then I'll send the pack down with Jake this morning. He says he's quitting anyways. He's downright sore about what happened yesterday. I guess I hadn't ought to have laughed so hard but doggone if I could help it. Makes me laugh still just thinking about it. He's crazy mad though, and I'll be glad to see him away from here. He might try some trick to get even. Why, he's even got it in for Philippa's pony."

"The idea! Poor Rico!" said Mrs. Pappadou.

"The other thing is," Jim went on, "do you want I should go, too? Mr. Simpson said you folks wanted to camp by yourselves for a while. If I go I'll have to take all the horses back—except Rico, of course. You'd be sort of marooned, wouldn't you? If anything happened, I mean. Anybody got sick or something."

"Would you be nervous, Mama?" asked Mr. Pappadou. He was thinking that they needed to be alone on Rico's account. But, on the other hand, if something happened, they would have no way of getting help. So finally they arranged for Jim to leave them, but to come back at intervals of a few days, bringing the mail and any fresh supplies they might need.

"Cindy and me can make the trip in a day easy," he said. "Well, O.K. then. I'll fetch in the horses and we'll get ready to leave. Anything you folks want in town, just give me a list."

· 140 ·

Mrs. Pappadou looked thoughtful.

"You know, I forgot my embroidery, Papa. I don't think I could ask Jim to buy me embroidery, even if they had the materials in Indian Springs, which I doubt. But if I had some paints, I could try to make designs of these pretty flowers, and embroider them afterwards. What do you think?"

Mr. Pappadou thought it was a very good idea. So she wrote "1 box of paints and brushes, 1 pad of white paper" on the list with the cocoa, sunburn oil, and peppermint lifesavers she also wanted.

Then Mr. Pappadou thought of something *he* wanted, and he gave Jim the names of three books about flowers of the Rocky Mountains which Tony Hartshorne had told him could be bought in Indian Springs.

Soon Jake rode off down the trail with the packhorses without a word of good-bye.

"Whew," breathed Mary Carey, "am I ever glad to see the last of that guy!"

Jim was tightening Cindy's girths while Chiquita, Freddy, Old Blue, and Three Cheers grazed nearby, ready to go.

"I left your saddle, Phil," said Jim, "is that right?"

"Oh goodness, yes!" cried Philippa.

Jim looked at Rico, standing tied nearby, but he didn't say anything.

"I'll be dreaming about those biscuits you're going to make me next trip," he told Mary Carey, as she handed him a trail lunch to put in his saddlebag. "Better practice up!"

"Does Sadie make good biscuits?" asked Philippa.

"Sadie? . . . What? . . . Oh, you mean *Sadie?* Oh sure. Of course. That is, she makes real powerful biscuits. We use them in sling-shots for huntin' ground squirrels. Nothin' better!"

"Oh, Jim!" Philippa laughed.

"Well, so long, folks." Jim vaulted onto Cindy without putting a foot in the stirrup, started the loose horses, and followed them down the trail, waving his hat and calling "See you Friday." He looked glued to the saddle as Cindy moved in her delicate running walk, prancing a little, neck arched and silky tail flying.

"Gosh, what a gorgeous mare!" sighed Mary Carey.

A long whinny from Rico seemed to agree with her.

Eleven

"Now, Rico, now!" cried Philippa as soon as Jim was out of sight. Rico was still whinnying and looking hopefully in the direction the horses had gone. He was lonesome.

"Don't cry, Rico!" said Philippa. "Cindy will come back." She stripped the blanket off and gave him a good grooming, combing out his mane and tail and smoothing the feathers in his wings.

"He begins to shine again, our beautiful Rico," said Mrs. Pappadou.

"He's still terribly thin," said Philippa, standing back and looking at him critically. "He isn't really strong yet. He'll need a lot of exercise before he's really strong, won't he, Mary Carey?"

"Yes," said Mary Carey, "and go slow at first."

Philippa saddled Rico and rode him at a walk once around the meadow. What a long time it seemed since she had been on his back!

The next day she walked him for nearly an hour and Rico was full of pep. He pranced the way he did when he wanted to fly, but Philippa held him down firmly. On the third day she trotted and cantered and he went so well that she rode up to the foot of the cliffs above camp, turned him toward home, and gave him the signal to take off. With an eager bound he sprang into the air, circled slowly once, and then sailed down to land beside Mary Carey, who was watching from the tents.

"That looked O.K.," said Mary Carey.

"It was just wonderful!" cried Philippa. "I'm going to do it again."

But Mary Carey thought that was enough for the first time. "And besides," she added, "today's Friday. Jim might arrive any time now."

When Jim did arrive, Rico was blanketed, standing hitched to a tree. He whinnied and pricked up his ears before anyone else was aware Jim was coming—Cindy's answering whinny from down the trail was the first they knew of it.

"Howdy, stranger!" called Mary Carey.

They were all glad to see Jim. He dismounted, dropping Cindy's bridle reins to the ground while he took mail and packages out of his saddlebags. Rico stretched forward as far as he could and touched noses with Cindy, the way horses do. Cindy laid back her ears and gave an indignant squeal, but the next moment they were touching noses again and from then on they seemed to relax and be friends.

"Rico's glad to have some company," said Philippa.

"He sure looks a whole lot better than he did," said Jim. "Seems like this mountain air does agree with him."

Mary Carey made the biscuits for supper, and Jim began by asking what brand of lead she used, but he ended up by saying they were really great, and ate five to prove it.

"Any news out in the big world?" asked Mr. Pappadou.

"Well, there's a circus coming to town," said Jim, "that's news in these parts. I don't remember a circus ever coming nearer than Basin City before."

"Ringling Brothers Barnum and Bailey?" asked Philippa, who went to the circus in the city every year.

"No, no. Nothing like that. Just a little one-ring outfit. Marples Mammoth Tent Show, it says on the posters. No great shakes, I guess. Oh, I saw those mountain climbers we met down at Camas Creek—Tony and what's-her-name . . . Lisa. They said they're aiming to try the northeast route up Myth soon again now."

"What about Jake Turpin?" asked Mrs. Pappadou. "Did he become more agreeable on the way home?"

"No, Ma'am," said Jim. "He didn't speak one word all the way to town. Except to tell me what he'd do to me if I was to mention what happened there at the ford."

"What did you say?" asked Philippa.

"I told him," said Jim, "I wouldn't hold a man up to public ridicule. But I told him I would have to warn Mr.

· 147 ·

Simpson that he was no man to work around dudes—too mean and ugly by far. He said I could tell Simpson anything I liked, he was quitting anyhow. He did, too—left town and hasn't been seen since."

"Good riddance to bad rubbish," said Mary Carey.

Jim left the next morning almost before daylight. Mary Carey crept out to make him some breakfast without waking Philippa. By the time Philippa woke up, he was gone.

In the next few days, Rico gained strength fast. Philippa flew him regularly morning and afternoon. First she stayed close to the meadow, circling low above the ground and landing often, sometimes coming down with a whirr of wings beside her Papa to see how he was getting along with his flowers, and sometimes to show her Mama, who was busy painting now, how well Rico was doing.

Sometimes she and Rico had a game with a fat, furry animal—Jim called it a hoary marmot—which liked to lie out on top of a rock near camp. If anyone came too near, the marmot gave a sharp whistle and ducked into his hole behind the rock. Philippa tried her best to swoop down on him unexpectedly from the air, but the marmot was always too quick for her, whistling and disappearing in a single instant. Then, as Rico streaked past, the marmot's head would poke out of the hole again to watch him go.

Gradually Philippa began to let Rico go higher. They flew along the cliffs of Myth Peak, so close that Philippa could see green and yellow lichens, like round splotches of paint on the rock walls, and tiny ledges where flowers bloomed in the sun, while around the corner on the same ledge, snow lay in shady crevices.

Once, passing a wider ledge, they startled some bighorn sheep—a ram and two ewes and a couple of half-grown lambs, coming on them so suddenly that Rico was startled, too, and shied in a great swerve that made Philippa thankful for her safety belt. The ram stood his ground, looking very noble with his huge curly horns lowered threateningly. But the ewes and lambs scrambled in panic, dislodging loose rocks that slipped and rolled and bounced off to drop a thousand feet or so.

Another time Philippa watched a white mountain goat lead her kid along a ledge so narrow that it looked like a crack in the cliff. At the end of it, where the wall became perfectly sheer, she jumped and landed neatly on a rocky platform many feet below, the kid following as perky and confident as if it were playing in a field instead of halfway up a precipice.

Sometimes they would disturb a hawk or an eagle from his perch on the cliff-face. The big birds, with their cold eyes and wicked talons, scared Philippa. They would flap screaming from their rocks as if they were about to attack her for daring to come near their private watchtowers. But Rico paid absolutely no attention to them. He swept by and away, and the birds, losing interest, circled back to settle on their perches again.

"CR-A-A-A-RRK!" The first time this unearthly croak sounded over Philippa's head she was terribly startled. A big black bird, like a huge crow, tumbled out of the sky almost on top of her, then slipped away sideways with hoarse cackles like laughing. There turned out to be lots of them around Myth Peak. They played in the wind, tumbling and swooping and chasing each other like clowns, letting off their funny creaky cries. She found out later from Jim they were ravens.

When she and Rico started chasing the ravens, they took it as a game and seemed to enjoy it. It got so every time Rico flew up from the meadows and began circling for altitude, ravens would flock from everywhere, rattling and crawking around them. Rico enjoyed it, too, but though he dived and side-slipped and zoomed like a stunt plane, the ravens were too quick for him. Philippa never could grab one—probably just as well, she decided, after a close look at the big birds' chisel-like bills.

After a good hard chase, Philippa would fly the panting Rico along the cliffs until she found a ledge wide enough and not too steep to land on. Then, while Rico foraged for harebells in the crevices of the rock, Philippa would settle herself in a comfortable seat and eat a cold flapjack and bacon saved from breakfast, or an almond Hershey bar.

As she sat there, she'd often remember the time she and Rico had landed on the balcony of the thirty-seventh floor of Metropolitan Towers.

"Do you remember how lonely it was, Rico? And there were millions of people there. Here it isn't lonely at all, and there's nobody! Why is that, I wonder?"

She would look down into the valley, thousands of feet below, with Myth Creek a blue thread squiggling in the bottom of it, and at the snow-streaked crags of the opposite mountains, and up at the precipice of Myth Peak towering above her, and at the precious dainty plants, like fairies' flower-beds, brightening the bare rock beside her—and would wonder if anybody, anywhere, had ever felt so happy.

Rico seemed happy, too. Nimble as the goat, graceful as the mountain sheep, and nobler even than the bighorn ram, he seemed as much a creature of the high peaks as they. Even more. For like the golden eagle, he was a creature of the wind and the sky besides.

"Oh, Rico!" Philippa cried. "I'm *never* going to let you go!"

She couldn't bear to think about it. She wouldn't think about it! Never. Never. NEVER!

"Come on, Rico, let's fly!"

Philippa mounted, fastened her belt, and touched Rico's flank with her heel. With an eager bound, the little horse sprang off the ledge, mane and tail flying, spread his wings as he began to drop, and a moment later soared in easy circles on the invisible currents of the air.

The first time Philippa went into a cloud she was good and scared. Rico was flying high, quite near the top of Myth Peak. Big, white, comfortable-looking clouds were drifting across, hiding the summits from time to time and dappling the lower slopes with swift-moving shadows. At one moment Philippa was in bright sunlight, looking at the far mountains melting away to blue haze under their broken roof of cloud, the next moment she was lost in a blank gray nowhere. The whole world was wiped out; she and Rico hung alone in a wet, chilling nothingness. Then suddenly they were out in the sun again, white cloud whirling away below them.

Nearby a jagged rock stuck up through the cloud like a reef from a scudding sea.

"The top of the mountain!" cried Philippa. Rico saw it, too. With powerful strokes he made headway toward it, rose slightly above it, and landed—not without a little scrambling and unsteadiness as the wind caught him before his wings were folded.

"Careful, Rico!" Philippa was a little frightened. But Rico, after a clatter and a clank, got his balance and stood steady on the tiny level spot that was the summit of Myth Peak. Somebody had built a little pile of stones there, and among the stones stuck a screw-top glass jar with a paper in it. Philippa would have liked to see what was written on the paper, but she didn't dare. There was barely room for Rico to stand—if she got off there might not be room for her. Or Rico might leave her. Her teeth chattered at the mere idea. As long as she stayed on Rico's back she wasn't a bit afraid—not of the height or the tearing wind, or even of the clouds. In fact it was glorious to be on top of the world. No wonder Lisa and Tony liked to climb here, though what hard work it must be compared to riding Rico!

Suddenly the clouds broke away all around her, and for the first time she could see the western side of the mountain. After a dizzy drop from the peak, so sheer that Philippa couldn't see the first thousand feet, snow fields and what looked like rumpled ice—a glacier?—slanted down to rocky ridges, under which cascades of broken rock fell to grassy slopes far, far below. These flattened out to a soft green bowl dotted with islands of trees and hemmed in all around by walls of rock. In the middle shone a little lake, a blue-green jewel of water, from which a thread of a stream wound its way to the only break in the surrounding wall, a narrow defile that, from the mountain top, seemed no more than a crack.

"It's Myth Valley!" cried Philippa. "It must be. Oh, Rico, doesn't it look lovely?" Rico, who had been winded when he reached the summit, was ready to go again now. He pawed restlessly.

"Shall we?" Philippa was tempted. Myth Valley looked so beautiful, so hidden and secret and enchanted.

But at that moment another big mass of cloud came blowing across, blotting out the valley and threatening to smother the summit again, and Philippa and Rico with it.

"Let's get away first," cried Philippa. Rico whirled and plunged off the summit ahead of the driving white billow. By the time the cloud swept past, they were out of its way.

"We'll go to Myth Valley tomorrow," said Philippa. "Too windy and cloudy today. But suppose we look for that pass on the way home, because that would be the easiest way."

So they flew to the left until they came to the lowest point between Myth Peak and the next mountain on the north. It was easy to see that this would be the only way into Myth Valley from this side. It did look steep—faint zigzags up a long slope of loose rock showed a trail of

sorts. But in other places, where rocky outcrops cut across the slope, no trail showed at all. Philippa wondered how an ordinary horse could ever get up such a place.

"But it won't bother us, will it, Rico?" It would be fun to go to Myth Valley. Philippa wondered why she hadn't thought of it before. It might be a terribly hard climb for an ordinary horse, but for Rico—why, by air, it was no distance at all from camp.

Twelve

Philippa was late for lunch. Mr. and Mrs. Pappadou seemed very serious, and even Mary Carey looked solemn, so Philippa said she was sorry she was late, and she didn't mention where she had been. But Mary Carey said it didn't matter, it was only sardine sandwiches, anyhow.

Then Philippa began to worry, because if it wasn't that, what was it?

She soon found out.

"Philippa, dear," said Mrs. Pappadou when they had all finished their sardine sandwiches, "your Papa and I would like to talk to you about something. Why don't we go and sit by the big rock where the view is and talk there. You come too, Mary Carey."

"O.K.," said Mary Carey, sounding cheerful, but looking as if she'd much rather not.

They all sat down by the rock. Mr. Pappadou put his arm around Philippa.

"Your Mama and I have been talking this morning," he said. "We think that we should be very happy. What we came here to do is done. Rico is well again—isn't that true, Philippa?"

Philippa's heart sank.

"Oh, Papa, I don't think he is quite well yet, not quite, really! He needs more time. Just a few weeks. Well, anyway, a few days. Oh please, please, not yet! Not yet!"

Mr. and Mrs. Pappadou looked sadly at each other. They had been dreading this moment when they would have to talk to Philippa about letting Rico go. Of course she would be upset—they would all miss Rico. But there was absolutely nothing else to do. They must take off his halter and let him fly back to where he came from. Taking him back to the city was out of the question. Mr. Olympio had certainly been very much mistaken when he thought that the roof of Metropolitan Towers was like a mountain. One must realize that since his retirement, Mr. Olympio had been very little in cities.

"Mr. Olympio said that they think it is good luck to have a horse like Rico," cried Philippa, "but this is the worst luck that ever happened!"

"Now see here, Phil, that's not fair!" said Mary Carey. "Look where we are. Would we be camping in the mountains if it hadn't been for Rico? Would we have come West at all, or seen all we've seen, or known Chiquita and Cindy and Three Cheers and Jim, or learned to make biscuits in a Dutch oven? Or found so many flowers? And would your Mama have found out she was an artist? You don't think it's good luck to have flown day after day over the city, to be the only little girl in the *world* to ride a pony with wings?"

"But if Rico goes, it's all over—things will be the same as always."

"No, Philippa," said Mrs. Pappadou, "I don't think things will ever be the same as always. We'll go home, but I think everything will be different."

"That's right," said Mr. Pappadou, "things are going to be different. I think I have not done well to spend so much time at my business. I am not going to work so hard any more, or worry so much. We will not have so much money, but we will have something better perhaps."

"Will we live in the country?" asked Philippa.

"I cannot promise that now," said Mr. Pappadou. "But one thing I do promise—we will come to the mountains again."

"Yes, Papa," said Mrs. Pappadou, "we must! We were not really living when we stayed in the city all the time. People need mountains. I have learned this."

"Now you see what Rico has done for you!" said Mary Carey. "You can't say he didn't bring you good luck. So how about thinking about Rico—what's best for him?"

Philippa didn't say anything. She knew what Mary Carey said was right.

"Well, we still have a few days," said Mrs. Pappadou. "You'll have time for more rides on Rico."

"I want to go to Myth Valley," said Philippa. "It's not a bit far—just over that low place between Myth Mountain and whatever that other one is called. That's Black Saturday Pass. I went to look at it this morning."

"Myth Valley is a place I'd like to see, too," said Mr. Pappadou, "but I'm afraid I cannot get there this time. The next time we come to the mountains, I shall certainly try to go."

"Please, may Rico and I go there tomorrow?" asked Philippa. "Then I can tell you what it is like."

Mrs. Pappadou did not like to have Philippa go so far out of sight of camp. But since there were so few days left for her to ride Rico, she finally agreed. Philippa promised to be very careful and not to be late getting back.

That afternoon Philippa rode Rico again, but the clouds were thick and the wind strong, so she did not go to the mountain. Instead, she flew out over the pointed treetops in the valley. The ravens found her there and joined in a game—they rejoiced in the blustery weather, skidding and tumbling in the wind like crazy children. Rico was full of pep in spite of his strenuous flight to the top of Myth Peak in the morning. But Philippa wished it was clear and calm—there was so little time left!

Alas, next morning the weather was even worse. Rain beat on the tents and thick clouds blotted out mountain and valley. The day after was a little better—the rain stopped, but clouds still hung low, at times even sagging down over the camp and the meadow. Philippa fidgeted and fretted.

On the third day it was still too foggy to go to Myth

Valley, but at least something happened—Jim came. He arrived riding a handsome big black horse. Philippa ran out to meet him.

"Hi, Jim," she called. "What horse is that? Where's Cindy?"

"This is Simpson's Black Magic," Jim said, dismounting and coming to the fire with mail and packages. "Cindy's missing."

"Missing?" Philippa and Mary Carey asked at once.

"Missing." Jim sounded gloomy. "I spent two days looking for her out in Mr. Simpson's big pasture, and all around it, too. She's hid on me before, but this time I think she's gone. She's just not there."

"Oh Jim, how terrible! What could have happened?"

"I don't know yet, but I aim to find out."

"Come and have some coffee," said Mary Carey. Jim handed Mr. Pappadou a bundle of letters and papers and went over to squat on his heel by the fire where Mary Carey was heating up the coffee pot.

"By the way," he said, "those mountain climbers—the Hartshornes—they finally got up Myth Peak by the Northeast Ridge. There's a piece in the paper about it. About three days ago—pretty near got into trouble coming down, too, weather turned real bad. But the funny thing is what they found on the top—read about it there—right on the front page."

"I bet it was a bottle," said Philippa. "There was a . . ." She stopped just in time.

"No, there's always a bottle or a can or something up there so's the climbers can write their names to prove they got there," said Jim. "No, it wasn't a bottle. It was a horseshoe."

"A horseshoe?"

"Read about it," said Jim.

Mr. Pappadou unfolded the paper. Right on the front page was a picture of Lisa and Tony with their ice-axes and packs, and a headline that read:

HORSE ON MYTH PEAK?

Two alpinists, Tony Hartshorne, 21, of San Francisco, and his wife, Lisa, 20, who succeeded in climbing Myth Peak yesterday by the difficult Northeast Ridge, report that they found a horseshoe on the summit.

Since the mountain can be scaled only by experienced climbers with alpine equipment, the find has aroused speculation locally.

"We would naturally have assumed that someone carried the shoe up and left it for a joke," Mr. Hartshorne stated, "except for one thing—there was a pile of horse dung there, too—and it was fresh. We didn't think anyone would carry a joke that far," he added.

The shoe is now on exhibition in the window of Mike's Mountain Supply on Main Street where it has been viewed by the large crowds in town for the circus.

Mr. Gus Marples, owner of Marples Mammoth Tent Show, now playing to capacity audiences here, has offered $10,000 cash for the horse which climbed Myth Peak.

"If there is such a horse," Mr. Marples said, "it belongs in Marples Mammoth Tent Show."

"Well!" said Mr. Pappadou, putting down the paper. "Well!" He didn't know what else to say. Philippa hadn't told them about flying to the top of Myth Peak, but from this it was clear that she had.

"Must be a hoax," said Mary Carey carelessly. "No horse could get up there."

Jim looked serious and also embarrassed.

"There's one thing I think I ought to tell you folks. I didn't mention this to nobody else, but I had a good look at the horseshoe in the window of Mike's Mountain Supply, and I recognized it. That's one of the little shoes I tacked onto Philippa's pony. That's Rico's shoe."

"How can you possibly tell one horseshoe from another," asked Mary Carey.

"Well, that set of shoes was a special small set Mr. Simpson brought back from Texas last winter. He sold the little pony they was meant for before he used them. They are different from the ones we use here—they were handmade for one thing. I'd have known them anywhere."

"Couldn't you be mistaken, Jim?" asked Mrs. Pappadou anxiously.

"I hardly think so, Ma'am," said Jim. "But of course there's a sure way to find out. If Rico still has all his four shoes, then I'm wrong."

The others exchanged glances. Philippa hadn't noticed, but she couldn't doubt it—Rico must have cast a shoe.

"I promised I wouldn't ask no questions," said Jim, "but I've been thinking plenty, and the only answer I can come up with is purely impossible. Ever since that pony crossed the creek without wetting hoof nor hair, I been trying to figure it out. Then leaving his shoe on Myth Peak, where even mountain climbers have trouble getting to. And now this—" he reached in his pocket and pulled out the broken tip of a silvery gray feather. "I found this down where I come out of the woods into the meadow. I've never seen such a big feather. No bird in these parts has feathers of the heft of that. No, sir, I'm not asking you, Mr. Pappadou—I'm telling you. Philippa's pony—I know it's impossible—but he must have—he's *got* to have—WINGS!"

"Yes, he has," said Mr. Pappadou. "You are perfectly right. He has wings. Come and sit down, Jim, and we will tell you all about it."

So they told Jim the whole story from beginning to end, and it was a relief to have him know. He promised not to say a word to a soul.

"Now would you like to see Rico fly?" asked Philippa, jumping up when they had finished.

"I *have* to see it," said Jim, "because I sure won't believe it until I do."

Philippa ran to where Rico was tethered and pulled off his blanket. Rico raised his wings as usual when the blanket was taken off, stretched and shook them, and settled them into place.

"I'll be . . . Of all the . . ." Jim could hardly speak. "It just can't be!" He stood with his mouth open and gaped at Rico. Rico pawed the ground restlessly. He wanted to go.

"If that isn't the purtiest thing I ever saw!" Jim got out at last.

Philippa saddled Rico and rode him out to the knoll in the meadow. As if he knew he was performing for a new admirer, Rico arched his neck and stepped sideways in his mincing, prancing way. Then, at Philippa's signal, he made a tremendous bound off the knoll, spread his big silver wings, and was airborne.

Jim gasped.

Philippa and Rico put on a regular air show for Jim. They did all the maneuvers and tricks they knew, including a game with a couple of ravens that volplaned down from the cliffs to join in the fun. Mary Carey finally had to go out and wave a dish towel to get them to come down.

Jim was terribly excited.

"What a cow pony he'd make! Especially in country like we have at the ranch. When one of those old cows takes her calf way up on the mountain, whish—up you go like a bird and land above her—no fighting your way up through the brush till your pony about breaks his lungs, or crashing down again over the rocks, risking his legs and your neck! Boy! It's a shame," he added, "he isn't a couple of sizes bigger."

"I know," sighed Mary Carey, "I've been wishing that ever since he came. I'd give about anything to ride him— even just one ride. But he's not up to my weight, let alone a man's."

Then an idea flashed into Mary Carey's mind.

"Jim—your ranch. Didn't you say it's a long way out—away off where people don't come much? You couldn't keep Rico for Philippa so she wouldn't have to let him go?"

Jim shook his head.

"I'd sure love to. But the fact of the matter is that the ranch has got to go, too. My Dad was doing all right, he was even going to expand and bring me in with him, until those Universal Development people started buying up all the land around us—land Dad has always leased for winter pasture. They won't renew the leases because they figure that if he goes broke they can buy his land, which they have to have if they're going to develop Myth Valley. He's dead set against selling out to those crooks, but I guess he's got no choice. It's about going to break his heart, too. If it wasn't for that, we might be able to keep Rico some way—at the ranch, or maybe up in Myth Valley."

Mary Carey was astonished. "Myth Valley? What do you mean, Jim? Is the man who controls—what is it called—Lost Canyon, what you were telling the Hartshornes about, is he . . . ?"

"He's my Dad, yes. And the old feller who found Myth Valley in the first place was my Dad's grandfather. Myth Ranch has been in the Randell family ever since then."

"I call it just a shame!" said Mary Carey. "A ranch that's belonged to so many grandfathers!"

"You're telling me," said Jim. "And all my life, I thought some day it was going to belong to me, too!"

Neither of them said anything after that. Jim kept

looking at Rico. He couldn't keep his eyes off him. Mary Carey wondered what he was thinking. She wondered if Jim was thinking about the $10,000 offered for the horse that lost a shoe on Myth Peak. There stood $10,000, which might be enough to save the ranch after all—anyhow, enough to buy a new one. And here it was, about to be turned loose—all that money just let go into the sky. It must make Jim feel bad, thought Mary Carey.

But then she felt ashamed for such a thought. Jim wouldn't even dream about selling something that wasn't his. And he would never be the means of shutting up a creature like Rico, away from the mountains and the sky, to starve in a grubby circus.

"Doggone," said Jim, "if that isn't the purtiest little animal!"

Thirteen

The next day—at last—was as fine a mountain day as anyone could wish for. It was their last day.

Philippa saddled Rico for the promised trip to Myth Valley—her last ride. Mary Carey put up some sandwiches and saw to it that she had an extra sweater and her slicker tied to the back of her saddle, for although the sun was bright in the bluest of blue skies, in the mountains you never can tell. Philippa promised her mother, who was nervous about her going so far, that she would not stay long, and that anyway, on Rico she was safe. Then she mounted and flew up toward Black Saturday Pass. The others stood by the tents and watched Rico's silvery wings flicker against the cliffs until they melted into the gray background. For a while Philippa's red shirt floated along like a separate bright spot, then it disappeared over the ridge.

It was such a glorious day, and she was so excited to be on her way to Myth Valley, that Philippa almost forgot that it was her last ride. As they flew low over the pass, Myth Peak towered above them on the left, a sharp, glittering spire from this angle, glorious in the early sun.

"See where we were, Rico!" Philippa talked out loud to Rico when they were flying. Rico didn't answer, but he was company, and she never felt lonely. She laughed to think how surprised the Hartshornes must have been to find that horseshoe. "They must have come right after we were there. If it hadn't been so cloudy, they might have seen us. I guess they'd have been even more surprised then!"

"Just think, Rico," Philippa went on. "You're wanted for the circus! I guess if that Mr. Marples knew what you can do, he'd have offered twenty thousand dollars instead of ten. But don't worry, if he had offered a hundred million, he couldn't have had you! . . . Still, wouldn't it be fun if we could both be in the circus, just for a while? I'd wear a gold spangled costume like the cowgirls in the rodeo, only much more glittery, and the lights would go down, and the band would play some airy music, and then suddenly a spotlight would shine out and there we'd be—circling round and round above the ring. And then we'd land and take a bow, and then I'd jump on your back and we'd fly around again amid terrific applause. Wouldn't that be really great? Shall we run away and join the circus, Rico?"

There was something about the shining air and the sky and the beckoning green of Myth Valley ahead that made Philippa think of all sorts of impossible things.

Why go back? Why shouldn't she stay here, and somehow fix it so she could keep Rico? She could live with Jim and his wife, Sadie, on Jim's father's ranch, which he said was way out somewhere in the mountains, away from town. School? No matter how far it was to school, she could get there on Rico even if the snow was ten feet deep. And Philippa saw herself, homework in one saddlebag, lunch in the other, commuting to school by air.

But it was time to pay attention to where she was going. The spruce-dotted meadows of Myth Valley were below her now, the lovely green-blue lake she had seen from the summit sparkled not far away. She decided to do the rest of her exploring on the ground.

Rico landed in a sea of flowers that made even Myth Meadows look poor.

She rode slowly through fields of Indian paintbrush of every shade, from palest yellow to orange to scarlet to rich maroon, bright blue penstemons, purple fringe, beargrass like snow-white sparklers, elephant heads, monkey flowers, asters, rosecrown. Rico snatched at the blue ones as he passed.

After a while they came to a place where ledges rose in rocky terraces at the upper end of the lake. Rico spread his wings and with an easy bound flew to the first rise.

Then he made his way up slowly from ledge to ledge, pausing every few steps to crop forget-me-nots and cushions of pale blue phlox. On these giant steps grew all of Mr. Pappadou's favorites, the exquisite little beauties that tuck themselves into cracks and corners or spread out in mats of color over the rocks: moss pinks and fairy primroses, snow buttercups, dryad, rock jasmine, dotted saxifrage. There were lovely blue columbines, mountain gentians, alpine asters, and where the snow-melt from slopes above ran down through spongy moss grew white marsh marigolds. It was the sweetest rock garden in the world, Philippa thought.

"Oh, if Papa could only see this!" cried Philippa aloud.

Everywhere she went there were flowers, and Rico was not alone in enjoying them, for twice she saw elk grazing, one a bull with magnificent great antlers; and another time several deer bounded away.

The trees grew in dark green islands among the flowery parks, their lower branches sweeping down around them like ladies' skirts, their tall spires pricking into the air.

On three sides, the valley was walled in by cliffs. On the fourth side—the east—the cliffs rose up to glittering snow fields and to the rumpled curl of a small glacier, which led in turn up, up, up to the rocky tower that was the summit of Myth Peak. The valley seemed a magic place, protected and closed in from all the rest of the world.

Philippa decided that her Papa and Mama must see this valley. They must come here next summer, no matter how rough and difficult the trail might be. She began to look for a nice camping place for them as she rode slowly around the lake.

At the lower end, the outlet tumbled and splashed through a bouldery bed which Rico cleared neatly, spreading his wings to carry him over. On the other side of this creek lay a level meadow with a view of the mountain, and another view of the mountain upside down, reflected in the lake. It was an ideal camping place.

"Whoa, Rico," said Philippa. "Look at that view, Rico!" She decided to eat her lunch here, and she got off.

When they stopped for lunch on the trail, Jim had loosened the horses' girths. Philippa wanted to do things right, so she loosened Rico's girth now. In fact, since the saddlepad was crooked, she took the saddle right off. It would give Rico's back a chance to cool. She took the bridle off, too, so he could graze without the bit, but she didn't let go of the lead-rope that was fastened to his halter. Though Rico had never failed to come when she called him, she felt much safer, somehow, if she had the rope in her hand.

So she sat down in the flowery grass and ate her sandwiches with one hand while she held Rico's rope in the other. She ate a little fast, because even if the sun is warm and the view is beautiful, it makes you feel funny to be all alone, the only person in a whole valley. Philippa wasn't scared, but she did feel funny.

Rico was hungry. He kept jerking the rope to get at flowers that were out of reach, so after she had finished her sandwiches, Philippa got up and walked after him, letting him graze wherever he pleased.

"Hurry up and eat, Rico," she said. "We mustn't stay too long."

But Rico seemed not to be able to get enough of the flowers of Myth Valley.

When Philippa was flying on Rico, time didn't matter and she never felt alone. But here on the ground, even in this heavenly place, she felt a little uneasy.

"Come on, let's go!" she said, pulling on the rope.

Rico lifted his head. Then suddenly his ears went up and he stood stiff with attention, staring across the meadow.

"What is it, Rico?" cried Philippa anxiously. "What do you see?"

Rico gave a loud, excited whinny and started forward, almost pulling the rope out of her hand.

"Whoa, Rico—stop!" Philippa braced herself and held the rope with both hands, but Rico dragged her along after him, whinnying again. Finally she tugged him to a stop. Then she looked up and saw what Rico saw.

It was a buckskin horse with a black mane and tail.

"Cindy!" cried Philippa. There was no mistaking the delicate head, the arched neck, and neat, rounded quarters—it was Cindy. She whinnied too, and galumphed toward them in an awkward canter. She was hobbled!

"Why Cindy! What are you doing here?" Philippa was dazed with astonishment. Rico asked no questions—he just acted delighted to see Cindy, who seemed even more delighted to see Rico. She came straight up to him and they touched noses in the most friendly manner.

Philippa tried to think. How in the world had Cindy got here? But she couldn't think of any answer to that question, so she thought about what she ought to do. There was only one thing she could do—saddle Rico and fly back as fast as possible to tell Jim where Cindy was. Jim would certainly be glad to know, and he would decide what to do about it.

"Good Cindy, good girl," Philippa held out her hand and Cindy put her nose into it. Philippa patted her neck. Then she turned Rico and started to lead him back to the place where she had left the saddle.

"Hold it!" rasped a creaky voice, "don't be in such a hurry, sister!"

"Oh!" Philippa whirled around, startled almost out of her wits.

There, not twenty feet away, looking at her with his crooked eyes, smiling his ugly smile, stood Jake Turpin.

"So that's it! Well, what do you know! I figgered it would be somethin' onusual, and I was right. I sure was right! A pony with wings, eh? Ha, ha. Old man Marples is goin' to get his money's worth sure enough. If I ever see a circus pony, this one's it."

"Oh, no. You can't . . ." began Philippa.

"Oh yes I can, little girl, and I'm a goin' to! No hollerin' and snivelin' is goin' to stand between me and ten thousand dollars, so save your breath. Just hand me that rope."

"Oh, but please listen, Mr. Turpin. Please! Rico can't live in a circus. He'd starve. He only eats flowers—flowers that grow in the mountains."

"Flowers that grow in the mountains, hey? Well, that's real purty, but it's not my problem. I'll have my cash in pocket and be on my way well before feeding time. Come on, now. No arguments."

"But he'll starve! He'll die! Don't you understand?"

"Hand me the rope! And if you try any monkey tricks, sister . . ." Turpin started angrily forward.

Philippa, so frightened she could hardly stand, threw both her arms around Rico's neck.

"No, no, NO!" she sobbed.

"Come on," growled Turpin, "that's enough."

He grabbed for the rope. Rico backed in alarm, twitching the loose end out of the man's reach. Still Philippa did not let go. Her arms were around Rico's neck, her fingers groping desperately for the halter buckle. With a curse, Turpin grabbed again, and as his hand closed on the rope he gave it a savage jerk.

"Oh no you don't, you don't get away that easy, circus pony," he rasped.

But he was wrong.

Jake Turpin held the rope in his hand, but it was slack. At the end of it, an empty golden halter lay on the ground.

"LOOK OUT!" cried Philippa, who had been thrown to one side the moment her fingers succeeded in unbuckling the halter.

Where Rico had stood, Philippa's sweet-tempered, obedient domestic pony, reared a wild creature with bared teeth and flaming eyes, whose wings whirred and clattered as he beat the air into a whirlwind.

"Oh!" cried Philippa and hid her face in her hands.

Rico sprang forward with a scream of rage that echoed round the cliffs, and immediately his cry was followed by another, hoarse and terrified, from Jake Turpin.

When Philippa dared to look up, Rico was high above her, circling in the peaceful air like a giant bird. On the ground nearby lay Jake, stretched at full length, groaning.

Philippa stood up, feeling dazed and lost, and looked around.

Then she picked up Rico's halter from the ground, though of what use could it be now? Here she was, grounded, miles from camp and from her mother and father, alone—well, not alone, but worse than alone. She hardly dared to look at the man who had caused this awful predicament. Suppose he was dead? Philippa shuddered with fear and horror.

But Jake Turpin wasn't dead. He was saying something. Cautiously Philippa moved a little closer. She could see that his eyes were open—his lips were moving.

"Help," he was muttering, "git help. Take the horse. Hurry!"

The horse? Cindy! She had forgotten all about Cindy. Where was she?

Looking around, Philippa caught sight of her a hundred yards away, snorting and panicky, as she hobbled around in circles staring at the sky. She was obviously as frightened by Rico's violent takeoff as Philippa had been.

"Can I catch her?" thought Philippa. Her legs felt weak as she walked uncertainly toward Cindy. She knew she couldn't catch her, even hobbled, unless Cindy would let herself be caught. She had come to Philippa and licked her hand when Rico was there, but now that Rico was gone and Cindy so frightened and nervous, could Philippa get near her?

"I must!" she whispered to herself. "I just absolutely must!"

If she could catch Cindy she could perhaps ride back over Black Saturday Pass to friends and safety. But if she couldn't? How would she ever walk so far? Dark would come, she'd lose her way—those slopes of sliding rock, those awful cliffs . . .

"Oh Cindy, come, please, please, please come!" Philippa walked slowly toward the little buckskin mare.

Cindy stood until Philippa was two arm lengths away. Then, as Philippa took one step nearer, the hobbles clanked and Cindy swung her head and forelegs around so that she faced away from Philippa.

"Whoa, girl," said Philippa softly, "whoa, Cindy." She circled slowly to approach Cindy's head again, talking gently all the time. Again Cindy moved out of reach with that fateful clank of the hobbles. But the third time, though her nostrils flared and her ears went back, she did not move as Philippa's hand went slowly forward and closed around the halter.

Cindy was caught!

The next thing was to get her back to where Rico's saddle lay on the ground and to get the saddle and bridle on her. Cindy was an altogether different kind of horse from Rico, and from steady old Three Cheers, too. She was jumpy and sudden. Philippa felt unsure about how to handle her. Until this desperate moment, it had never occurred to her that she *could* handle her.

But now she had to.

"Come on, Cindy—!" Philippa did not dare take off the hobbles until she had Cindy bridled and tied up. So she pulled on the halter and coaxed and persuaded Cindy to move toward the saddle. Walking with the short little steps which were all the hobbles allowed, it took a long time. Cindy tossed her head with impatience, threatening to pull away, but Philippa hung on for dear life.

They finally reached the place where the saddle and bridle lay on the ground where she had thrown them when she stopped for lunch—how long ago? Less than an hour, perhaps, but it seemed to Philippa as if it must have been in another lifetime.

Rico's bridle was too small for Cindy—it pulled up the sides of her mouth and made her champ irritably. Philippa let it out to the last hole. Though it was still a little too tight, it would have to do.

She tied Cindy firmly to a tree while she put on the saddle. The saddle girth was too short, but Philippa knew how to let it out and adjust it on the off side, and she pulled it up as tight as she could. Then she unbuckled the hobbles.

The next thing was to get on. Cindy was not a big horse, but she was quite a lot higher than Rico. Three Cheers had been about the same size, but Jim had usually given Philippa a leg up, or led Three Cheers to a log to make mounting easier. Would Cindy go up to a log and stand still to let her get on?

There were no logs nearby, but there were lots of rocks. Philippa led Cindy up to one. The little mare stood still until Philippa got up on the rock, but then she swung around and faced Philippa, putting the stirrup hopelessly out of reach.

"Oh Cindy, don't!" cried Philippa. She tried again. Again Cindy stood sideways to the rock until Philippa climbed up on it, but quickly swung around before she could get her foot in the stirrup.

The harder Philippa tried, the worse Cindy behaved. She finally refused to go anywhere near the rock. She seemed to be growing more obstinate and irritable every minute. Philippa, beginning to be afraid of her, was near to despair.

Then suddenly Cindy stopped fidgeting and stood stock-still, as still as a statue, looking fixedly toward the mountain. As it happened, she was standing where the ground sloped a little, so that Philippa had the advantage of being on the uphill side. Her foot just reached the stirrup, her hands grasped the pommel and the cantle, and with the strength of sheer desperation, she hauled herself onto Cindy's back.

Still Cindy didn't move, though as Philippa settled herself, she felt a sort of quiver go through Cindy's body.

"What is it, Cindy? Whoa, now. Please be good!" Philippa was still breathless. She had tight hold of the pommel and held the reins short. Cindy felt like coiled springs, ready to let go. Philippa's heart was in her mouth.

Then glancing up quickly, she saw what Cindy was

looking at—far up toward the mountain, flashing in the sunlight as it wheeled, wild and free and beautiful, flew a great bird. No, of course it wasn't a bird—it was Rico!

Rico! Philippa had not had time to think of him since the moment when her terrified fingers unfastened his golden halter. If she had thought of him at all, it was only that he was gone, lost, forever lost and gone.

And now, there he was, lazily circling over the snow in the noon sunlight.

Cindy gave a short excited whinny and bounded forward so suddenly that Philippa nearly lost her seat. Then before she was back in the saddle, they bore down at a canter on the place where Jake lay in the grass. The injured man raised himself on one elbow, gesturing feebly, and Cindy shied with a tremendous swerve. Poor Philippa! She flew so far into the air that her hands clenched on the pommel were her only contact with the saddle. Somehow she managed to stay on until at last she scrambled back into balance and found her stirrups and got some sort of control over the reins.

She had one glimpse of Jake's crooked face. A hoarse wail of "Help!" trailed after her up the valley.

No doubt about it, Jim spoke the truth when he said Cindy was too much horse for Philippa. There was no controlling her. If Philippa pulled hard on the reins, Cindy slowed up in short, jarring jumps, throwing her head up and down and gathering herself to go faster as soon as the reins loosened.

Philippa was soon breathless, her legs ached, her arms felt limp, and she was scared clear through. One single idea possessed her—to stay on. No matter how fast, how rough, how uncontrollable Cindy was, she must stick to her.

One thing began to be clear—Cindy knew where she was going. She was skirting back along the lake on the opposite side from the one Philippa had taken, the side nearest to Black Saturday Pass. Presently, Philippa could see they were on a trail. In a low place, where they crossed a tiny stream, she realized (when she'd recovered from the long flying jump with which Cindy cleared it) that there had been horse tracks in the wet mud. From then on, wherever they passed through a narrow opening between trees or rocks, there was a definite track. In any case, they were headed for the north side of Myth Peak and Black Saturday Pass—the right direction. But Philippa was beginning to be giddy.

"Oh Cindy, whoa . . . I can't, I just can't . . ." She gave a despairing pull on the reins, her last ounce of strength, and suddenly, Cindy slowed to a walk. She was panting hard, sides heaving, sweat lathering her neck. The way had now begun to go steeply uphill. From here on Cindy went quietly and Philippa was able to relax her aching muscles and try to gather her wits.

She could now see that there really was a trail, and that a horse had recently come down it—Cindy with Jake probably, coming in. Jake must have taken Cindy out of Mr. Simpson's pasture—stolen her! And he intended to steal Rico to sell him to the circus. And if Rico hadn't struck Jake in his mad plunge to go free, Jake would be the one riding Cindy out of Myth Valley right now, leading Rico.

"He'd just have left me there all alone, I know he would," thought Philippa with a shiver. "If he was mean enough to do what he did, he'd be mean enough to leave me all by myself in the valley. You shouldn't be glad when people are hurt, but I'm not a bit sorry about him. Of course, I'll tell Jim, and he'll send help or something. Oh dear, if I ever do get back to Jim, and to Mama and Papa . . ."

Philippa began to feel tears coming. The way up to Black Saturday Pass began to look steeper and scarier the closer she got to it. From Rico's back, high up above, it hadn't looked very long or particularly hard. They had soared over in a few minutes. How different to be grounded, to have to labor up endless zigzags, foot by weary foot. Worse, Philippa remembered what Jim had said—it was a difficult, dangerous pass, even for Cindy.

"Oh Cindy!" Poor Philippa talked aloud the way she used to talk to Rico. "Please Cindy, be careful! Please take me home, oh, take me home!"

But even Cindy's spirits seemed to be flagging. The climb was telling on her, and as she stopped to pant for breath, Philippa put her face down onto the silky mane and began to cry.

Suddenly Cindy lifted her head, bumping Philippa in the forehead, and gave a sharp, startling whinny. Then she jerked forward, climbing with a new burst of speed.

Philippa looked up. There on a rocky promontory high

above, outlined against the sky, stood a horse.

It was Rico!

For some reason the sight of Rico cheered Philippa, and it certainly put new life into Cindy. He couldn't help them now—he was no more use than a mountain goat or a bighorn ram. Indeed, that's all he was now, just another wild animal. But he was a living creature and he was watching them intently. This frightening wilderness of rock and snow seemed less lonely because of him.

Philippa's hand felt for the golden halter tied to her saddle.

"If he would just wait," she thought with a rush of hope, "if I could just get near enough!"

But the hope died as they finally scrambled to the level where Rico stood. For a moment it looked as if he would come forward to meet Cindy and touch noses the way they used to do. But when Philippa moved her hand to untie the halter, Rico reared, wheeled, and sprang into the air with a snort of alarm. In a moment he was soaring out over the valley, half a mile away.

Still, he didn't disappear altogether. All through the weary hours that Cindy labored up the switchbacks of Black Saturday Pass, Rico stayed in sight. Sometimes he was just a speck in the sky far above the summit, visible only when the underside of his wings caught the sun; sometimes he circled down and landed above them, knocking off loose rocks that bounced and rattled past them. He folded his wings and stood watching their slow, painful climb.

The trail across the pitches of slipping, sliding rock

was hardly a trail at all, and it grew steeper and steeper. In places it threaded between precipitous outcrops, one above, one below, on a slant so sharp that it didn't seem believable that Cindy could keep her footing—places where it would be impossible to turn around if she made a mistake in choosing her way. Philippa hung onto the pommel, trying not to look down, tired and giddy and scared to death. Her eyes clung to Rico, always somewhere above them, as if the sight of him were all the hope she had.

Again and again Rico stood on what she felt sure must be the top of the pass, flying off just before Cindy reached it. Again and again, when they had panted to the hoped-for summit, there was another even steeper slope looming ahead.

They reached a place where Cindy stopped short at a pitch of almost sheer rock, covered with treacherous loose gravel. The cracks running across the face of the outcrop would scarcely make toeholds for a man to climb. How could Cindy possibly get up such a place as that? Below, a slide of loose stones sloped to a sheer drop of a hundred feet. Even turning around looked impossible.

"If I could just get off," thought Philippa. But there was not room to get off.

At that moment Rico, who stood watching them as usual from a ledge above, suddenly turned his head to look behind him at something. Then he wheeled around, ears up, alarmed, as if danger threatened from that direction. In another instant he plunged away in panic, mane and tail flying, wings beating with frantic strokes.

Before Philippa could wonder what had frightened him, Cindy lurched forward, scrambling, scraping, digging in her toes, with heart-stopping slips on the loose gravel, with heaving and panting and straining every muscle under her sweat-soaked hide, she got herself and Philippa up the impossible pitch. For long minutes the little mare stood with trembling legs, gasping for breath. Finally with a sigh, she started up again and went on without trouble to the next rise.

There ahead of them—at last—Philippa could see the whole line of the northeast ridge, and the low spot between Myth and Marvel Peaks that was the pass. It didn't look too far, and it didn't look too steep, but the whole distance between her and the top of the pass was covered with snow.

Snow!

Jim had said that the pass was often blocked with snow. Was it blocked now? Could Cindy cross it? Or would she sink in and be unable to move? Cold despair filled Philippa at any thought of turning back. She couldn't—she just *couldn't*—go back down that terrible trail.

But did she dare ride across the snow? Was it safe for horses?

Suddenly Cindy whinnied, a loud, shrill whinny that shook her whole body, and Philippa too, body and nerve. The startling sound echoed from cliff to cliff in weird dying cries.

"Oh Cindy," cried Philippa. "Oh, why did you scare

me so? What is it?" She looked around for Rico, but he was nowhere in sight.

Then she heard something—not an echo, not a whinny, but a shout—a human person's shout. Again. And then a far-off whinny, too. And then she saw them—just below the pass, making their way in single file across the snow—horses, one, two, three—two of them with riders.

Cindy whinnied again and set off briskly across the snow—it was quite hard, she didn't sink in—and Philippa saw that there were tracks in it which she had not noticed at first. In a few minutes she could hear the shouting plainly: "Phil-*lip*-pa!"

They were looking for her!

In another few minutes she could make out the riders: Papa, on Freddy, Jim on the big stallion, Black Magic. Jim was leading Three Cheers.

"Papa, Papa, Papa!"

A few minutes more and her Papa was hugging her tight.

"I found Cindy," she explained to Jim after a while, "and I had to let Rico go. But he didn't go right away. He's still around here. Oh Papa, so much happened."

"You can tell us all about it later, sweetheart," said Papa.

"We saw Rico," said Jim, "that's why we came. When we saw him flying around loose and on his own, we didn't waste any time."

"We must hurry to get back to Mama," said Mr. Pappadou. "She is waiting with Mary Carey at the top of the pass. She is very frightened."

"Oh dear, poor Mama," cried Philippa. "Let's hurry!" But when Philippa tried to hurry she found she felt wobbly all over. Jim held her up.

"How about you riding with me?" he said, and he swung her into his saddle on Black Magic and mounted behind her. It felt good to lean back against Jim's hard chest, with his strong arms holding her safe, and let him do all the riding and the thinking. Papa was right there behind, with Cindy and Three Cheers bringing up the rear as they plodded back up the snow toward the top of Black Saturday Pass.

"Oh Jim," sighed Philippa. "I'm so glad you and Papa came! I didn't think Cindy would ever . . ." Suddenly, she sat up stiff and straight—so suddenly that Jim got a sharp jolt on the chin from the top of her head.

"I forgot!" she cried. "Jim, somebody has got to do something!"

"Do what?" asked Jim. "Don't worry yourself, Phil. If there's something to do, we'll do it later. Take it easy, now."

"No, no, he's hurt!" insisted Philippa. "He's hurt! He's bad and I hate him, but he's hurt. He's just lying there."

"Who?" asked Jim. "What do you mean?"

"Jake," said Philippa.

"Jake Turpin?"

"Yes. He's there. That's why I let Rico go. Jake tried to take Rico for the circus—for that money, you know—.

He took Cindy, too. Oh Jim, it was awful!"

"Jake Turpin!" cried Jim again. "That—that low-down, lousy . . ."

"He's horrible," said Philippa, "but he's hurt. Rico knocked him down and he can't get up."

"Serves him right!" said Jim, angrily. "So now," he went on, "we got to ride all the way down and bring out that no-account trash."

Philippa shivered. She remember how close she'd come to being the one left alone in Myth Valley.

"Oh well, you relax, kid," said Jim more cheerfully. "We'll take care of it. Look who's up there. See your Ma and Mary Carey?"

Sure enough, perched on the rocks at the top of the pass, Philippa could make out two anxious figures watching and waving as the horses plodded toward them.

Presently Black Magic's hoofs crunched on rock, the trail reappeared from under the snow, and a few minutes later, Jim lowered Philippa into her mother's arms.

Fourteen

By the time Philippa had had a drink of hot tea that Mary Carey had brought in a thermos, and a sandwich and a chocolate bar, she was feeling a lot less wobbly, and she was able to give a more or less connected account of what had happened to her in Myth Valley. Mrs. Pappadou exclaimed in horror. Mary Carey kept saying "Jeepers!" in the most admiring way.

"If you could just have seen Rico, Mary Carey—all of a sudden he was so changed! He was like . . . like a dragon! But he didn't fly straight away, that's the funny thing."

"I know," said Mary Carey, "we saw him. He was flying slowly in circles. And when we saw you weren't on

his back, and no saddle, and no halter—well, we just about died!"

"I did die," said Mrs. Pappadou. "My heart stopped beating!"

"Oh Mama!" Philippa gave her a hug. "It's all right now. Cindy brought me back." Philippa was beginning to feel pleased about riding Cindy. "Gee, Mary Carey, flying on Rico didn't feel as fast as Cindy. I just about couldn't even breathe!"

"I'll bet," said Mary Carey, admiringly. "I never would have thought you could do it. You're a sure enough cowgirl, no fooling."

"I had to," said Philippa.

Mr. Pappadou and Jim, standing over beyond the horses, out of hearing of the others, were talking.

"If the packtrain had've showed up," said Jim, "there'd be no problem. I'd take José and leave Clem to pack up for you folks and guide you down. He could do it easy, especially with Mary Carey to help—she's getting to be as good as another wrangler. But they must've got hung up somewhere or something. I don't dare wait any longer to get down the pass. Philippa's right, it's a tough trail and besides, I want it to be daylight when I'm looking for that son of a gun in the valley."

"I don't like your going alone, Jim," said Mr. Pappadou. "With a bad trail and a bad man at the end of it, you shouldn't go alone. It's taking too much of a chance."

"Oh, that's O.K.," said Jim. "I'll be real careful. I

guess I can handle Turpin. After all, Mary Carey did."
He smiled.

But Mr. Pappadou wouldn't give in. For a man who
hadn't ever been a very adventurous kind of man, he was
quite firm about going.

"I'm going with you," he said. "Mary Carey, are there
any sandwiches left? Give us all the food you brought
along. And you and Mama take Philippa back to camp.
The trail isn't too bad on this side."

"Oh sure," said Mary Carey. "We can get back O.K."

"Papa—what? Where are you going?" cried Mrs.
Pappadou.

"Now, Mama, it's all right." Mr. Pappadou settled his
hat on his head. "I am going with Jim to get this Jake
Turpin, who is a bad man, but after all, a human being.
He cannot be left to die alone in the mountains. We will
go down into Myth Valley the way Philippa came up—
the way Jake himself went down, several days ago. But
Jim says we will go out the other way—toward the west, a
trail through a canyon which Jim knows well and which
leads to Jim's father's ranch, near a place call Lariat. So
then we can arrange to turn Turpin over to the proper
authorities and send for a car to take me around to meet
you at Indian Springs. You should reach there tomorrow
night at the latest, if you make the trip in one day. Jim
thinks we should get there by then, in plenty of time to
catch our plane."

"But Papa . . ."

"Now, Mama, it is all right. I'm going with Jim. It is

decided." Papa walked over to Freddy and ran his hand under the girth to see if it was tight. He did it as if he'd been testing saddle girths all his life.

Mrs. Pappadou knew that when Mr. Pappadou said in that tone of voice that a thing was decided—the thing was decided.

Jim tightened all the other girths, gave Mary Carey a lot of directions, and told her what to tell Clem when he and José arrived with the packhorses that evening. Then he lifted Philippa into her own saddle on Cindy's back.

"I guess you can ride Cindy back to camp or anywhere else now, can't you, Phil?" Philippa said she guessed she could. Cindy was standing very quiet, with lowered head, her coat rough and wispy with dried sweat. She didn't look as if she would give Philippa any more trouble this day.

"Well, so long," said Jim. "Take care now, girls. It's been real nice to know you."

"Oh, Jim," cried Philippa. "We're going to see you again, aren't we?"

"No, I reckon it's good-bye," said Jim. "By the time I get back around the mountains with the horses, you'll all be gone." Jim looked sad, too.

"Oh dear!" cried Philippa. "Oh Jim, I don't want to say good-bye!"

"Nor me either, I sure don't, kid. But that's the way it is." He shook her hand. Then he walked over and shook Mary Carey's. Mary Carey said, "Good-bye, Jim."

"Jim," said Mrs. Pappadou. "We'll never, never forget

you. You made everything so happy for us. Thank you, dear Jim!"

"Thank *you*, Ma'am," said Jim. "I'm sure I won't never forget you folks, neither. And Rico, too!"

"Come on, Jim," called Mr. Pappadou. "We should start now."

Jim swung into the saddle, and, leading Three Cheers, who was to carry the wounded man, the two men started down toward Myth Valley far below.

"Be careful, Papa!" pleaded Mrs. Pappadou, waving. Mr. Pappadou smiled and waved back with his big hat.

"He should have let me go," said Mary Carey.

"He wouldn't because he wanted to go himself," said Mrs. Pappadou, sighing. Mary Carey sighed, too.

But now Mary Carey was the leader—it was no time to sigh. She must get Philippa and her mother safely back to camp.

"Come on," she said. "I'll go ahead. Phil, you come after me, and Mrs. P. behind you so she can see if you begin to look wobbly."

But Philippa didn't feel so wobbly now, only let down and limp and sad. As they zigzagged down from Black Saturday Pass, Myth Peak cut off the westering sun and they seemed to be sinking deeper and deeper into the gloom. Jim was gone, Papa too. Mama was worrying so hard about Papa that you could feel the air thick with worry. And tomorrow they would be leaving the mountains. Everything was over—troubled and unhappy and over. And worst of all, Rico was gone!

They rode slowly down, down, down. As they neared camp, the cliffs of Myth Peak, the opposite mountains, the shadowy spruce-filled valley, all seemed gradually to rearrange themselves and take the familiar shapes and outlines Philippa knew so well. Now every crack on the cliff-face, every patch of snow and pinnacle of rock was familiar, and spoke to her of Rico.

Oh Rico! How could she live without him?

They rode forlornly into their empty camp. Nothing is so sad as a happy place from which the joy has gone. When they passed the trampled spot where Rico used to stand, where his blanket still hung on a branch, Philippa thought her heart would break.

"Heavens to Betsy!" cried Mary Carey. "Look, look, Philippa! Look!" At the same moment, Cindy lifted her tired head and gave a long whinny.

Out of the sky came a wild shrill answer.

Philippa looked up. There, in a shaft of sunlight that spilled across the ridge from the west, soaring in long lazy circles, flew Rico.

Philippa had never seen Rico fly until today. The sight of him now, shining against the shadowy mountain, took her breath away. He was so beautiful, so wild and free and beautiful. Her heart filled with joy as she watched him. Round and round he flew, higher and higher as the light withdrew, until he was a glowing speck in the sunset sky above the mountain.

They were still looking when there came a clatter and hallooing from down the trail. The packtrain was coming. When Philippa looked up again, Rico was gone.

"Hi!" called a cheery voice. "Afraid we're kind of late. Where's Jim? I'm Clem Hicks."

Clem was a nice-looking man, big and strong, with smile-crinkles in the corners of his eyes. He looked so much like everybody's idea of a cowboy that Philippa's hopes for Mary Carey rose once more. Perhaps, even at this late date . . . But when Clem raised his curly-brimmed hat she saw there were threads of white in his thick black hair. No, he was too old. Even if he had a ranch, he'd be sure to be married already.

"This is José Vargas," Clem said.

Philippa turned around to look at the other rider. She got a flashing smile and a friendly "hello" from José, who was slight and boyish, with melting black eyes in his round brown face. He looked about seventeen.

"Hi," said Philippa and tried to smile back, but her smile faded into disappointment. José wouldn't do either—he looked nice but he was too young.

"You folks just back from a ride?" asked Clem. "Where's Jim?"

Mary Carey explained that Jim had taken Mr. Pappadou over to see Myth Valley and that they were going out the other way. She gave him all Jim's directions.

"If you'll take care of these horses," she said, "I'll see about supper."

"Supper is a word with real appeal to José and me right now," said Clem. "Leave the horses to us. Say," he went on, surprised, "isn't this Jim's mare? Sure, this is Jim's buckskin, the one he sets such store on. He was looking all over for her back a few days. Thought she'd been stole or something. Well, I'm glad he found her. You must be in his special good books, sister, if he lets you ride that mare. And a pretty darn good rider, too. I'm surprised. What I mean, that's no dude horse."

"Come Philippa," interrupted Mrs. Pappadou. "You can talk to Clem tomorrow. She's had a hard day," she explained to Clem as she led Philippa away.

"Looks like the mare's had a hard day, too," said Clem. But he never heard why Philippa and Cindy were both so tired. They had all decided to say nothing to anyone about what happened in Myth Valley.

"If we can make a real early start," said Clem after supper, "we can get all the way down tomorrow."

"Oh yes, that is what we must do," said Mrs. Pappadou, who would go on worrying every single instant until she saw Mr. Pappadou again, or at least until she knew he was safe back from Myth Valley.

But they didn't make an early start.

About dawn the next morning, there was an unusual commotion out on the meadows where the horses, belled and hobbled, had been driven to graze the night before— a great thudding and neighing and frantic jangling of bells, and then the whole lot of them came clumping into camp in a sort of stampede as if they were frightened. José ran out among them, calling to calm them, catching the leaders and heading off the ones that seemed bound for the homeward trail. Before long, all the horses were tied up—all, that is, but Cindy.

"That buckskin mare of Jim's seems to be missing," said Clem. "What's the matter with that nag, anyhow? Ride out and see if you can find her, José."

So José rode out and searched the meadows up and down. Mary Carey had cooked and served breakfast and washed most of the dishes before he got back. He didn't have Cindy.

"Well, we'll go ahead and pack up," said Clem, "and try to leave an extra packhorse over for the little girl to ride. Jim'll be fit to be tied if we don't bring in that mare, though."

"We just can't go back without Cindy," cried Philippa.

"Oh, I did so want to start early so we can reach town tonight," said Mrs. Pappadou. "I'm so worried about Papa. Oh dear, why did Cindy have to get lost!"

"I'm going to go and look for her," announced Philippa. Mrs. Pappadou didn't want her to go, but she did understand how important it was to try to find Cindy.

"Don't *please* go too far, dear. Be very careful. Don't climb too high, will you? Come back if you don't find her quite soon."

Philippa promised. She left the sad bustle of breaking camp and walked out to the meadows. She climbed the flowery slope she used to ride up to her takeoff knoll, past the knoll and on to the steeper slopes, where there was such a glorious view of the peaks across the valley, and such a clear view of the whole of Myth Meadows. Surely Cindy *must* be there—where else could she be? Philippa sat down on a rock to look.

The meadows stretched up to the foot of the cliff,

empty and lifeless. Even the big marmot was absent from his lookout rock. As Philippa's eye traveled along the familiar cliffs, something caught her attention—something moved on one of the narrow ledges where she had often landed Rico. A sheep? A goat? No! It was Rico himself! When he stood still against the weathered rock, wings folded, it was almost impossible to see him. Now she realized what Papa meant by "protective coloration" and what Mary Carey meant by "camouflage": the silvery gray feathers of his folded wings, the broken pattern of his gray and white markings, made him practically invisible.

So he was still here! He still had not flown away to his home across the sea.

"Rico," called Philippa, with sudden hope, and she tried to whistle the way she used to when she wanted him to come. The whistle came out dry and feeble. But Rico heard her. He turned his head, and when he suddenly launched himself from the ledge, she thought: "He's coming!"

But he didn't come. Instead, he flew with rapid strokes away from her along the cliff and landed again further off—melting into invisibility the moment he stopped moving.

Philippa sighed. Somehow she didn't feel so badly about Rico now. He was still here, that was something. But clearly he didn't belong to her anymore; he belonged to the mountains, like the sheep and the eagles and the big whistling marmot, and all the other wild animals.

People who love a place begin to feel as if they own that place. Philippa already felt that way about Myth

Meadows and Myth Peak and everything belonging to them. And since Rico belonged to them now, Rico was still—in a way—hers, too. Not that Philippa thought this all out in words—just that she began to feel happier about Rico, as if, after all, it was more right for him to be free.

As she sat looking at the spot where she knew Rico was, even if she couldn't see him, he suddenly flew again. He circled slowly down to the foot of the cliff and landed in the meadow. It was a long way off, but she could see him now, and as she watched the spot, another animal moved out from an island of bushy spruces—another horse. It looked like . . . it must be . . . it was . . . Cindy! She and Rico met, touched noses, and fell to grazing side by side.

Philippa jumped up.

She must run back to camp and tell José, who would ride out and bring Cindy in. But what if he saw Rico? Philippa remembered the trouble that followed when people saw Rico. And then there was that reward—the thought of it made her shudder. No. She would have to see if she could get Cindy herself.

Cindy was at last led into camp, but not by Philippa.

When Philippa finally got near the two grazing horses, Rico took off like a startled bird. And Cindy took off, too. Even hobbled, she could canter at a good clip. She would stop to graze, one eye warily on Philippa, but no matter how Philippa coaxed and wheedled and moved softly, before her outstretched hand could reach the halter, Cindy would jerk up her head and clank away.

Finally, José had to come out and rope her. Philippa kept an anxious watch on the cliffs, but if Rico was there, he didn't show himself.

All this took a long while. By the time Cindy was saddled and ready, it was very late.

"Doggone you, Cindy," said Clem, "what makes you so contrary? Now we're going to be late as blazes getting into town tonight."

As it turned out, they didn't get into town that night at all.

One thing after another delayed them. First, Mrs. Pappadou remembered, after they had been on the trail nearly half an hour, that she'd left the canvas bag with her paintbox and the sketchbook with all her flower pictures out by the view rock. José went back and couldn't find it, so then she had to go herself. Then one of the packhorses stepped on a ground hornet's nest, and by the time he'd finished bucking and plunging around, he had to be repacked. The Myth Creek ford was even deeper and wilder than when they had come in—it took quite a while to get all the horses, not to mention Mrs. Pappadou, safely across. When they had to stop for lunch far short of Camas Creek, where they'd spent their first night, Clem discovered that Old Blue had cast a shoe. She was favoring her near front foot. That meant rummaging around in the pack for the shoeing equipment and another delay. By the time they reached Camas Creek it was late afternoon, and it looked like rain.

"Ma'am," said Clem, "we can get in tonight, but I'm afraid it will be pretty dark and late before we do."

"Oh dear," said Mrs. Pappadou, who had set her heart on being in town where she could at least be near a telephone in case there was a message from Mr. Pappadou. "Oh dear, Clem, I do want to go on."

"It's all right with me, Ma'am," said Clem, "if you and Mary Carey and the little girl won't get too tired."

Mrs. Pappadou, who was too tired now, said of course she wasn't a bit, and that nothing could tire out Mary Carey. But then she looked at Philippa and remembered what the child had been through the day before.

"Seems a little green around the gills," whispered Mary Carey. "I think she's had it for today, Mrs. P."

Mrs. Pappadou looked at Philippa's white face and thought so, too.

So they stayed.

The horses were no sooner unpacked and the tents put up than a steady drizzle set in. Clem and José rigged a tarpaulin and split some wood for the cook-fire, and Mary Carey started a pot of water for tea. Philippa crawled into her sleeping bag without a fuss when her mother urged her to rest. Nobody talked much. It was cold, clouds shut out the view, the rain pattered on the tent.

"Ow! Drat!" exclaimed Mary Carey, as a little stream of cold rain water dribbled off the edge of the tarpaulin and ran down the back of her neck. Clem, squatting on his heel to fan the reluctant fire with his hat, looked at her with a wry expression.

"Well, anyway, it's Western," he said.

The kettle boiled at last.

"Gee, it seems a lot different from the last time we

camped here, doesn't it?" said Mary Carey, coming into the tent with two steaming cups of tea.

"It is certainly very different," sighed poor Mrs. Pappadou, and then in a low voice so Philippa wouldn't hear—"I wouldn't mind the rain or the cold—but oh, Mary Carey, I am so frightened about what may have happened to Papa in that valley—that terrible man—it's so awful not to know. If we could have reached town tonight . . . Mercy goodness! What was that?"

Out of the darkness and rain, quavered a long, blood-curdling whoop: "Yeeeeeee-hooooooooo!"

Clem and José, out by the horses, suddenly raised their voices, but Mary Carey and Mrs. Pappadou couldn't understand what they were saying.

Again the outlandish yell, and a sound of horses' hoofs. Mary Carey crawled out of the tent.

"Someone's coming," she said. "Clem and José know who it is. It's a man on a horse—nothing to worry about, I guess. Well, glory be!—it's JIM!"

"Jim!" cried Mrs. Pappadou.

"*Jim!*" cried Philippa, bouncing out of her sleeping bag and out into the rain that didn't seem to matter any more.

"I had a hunch you folks wouldn't make it down in one day, so I just come up to meet you," said Jim, dismounting. "Mr. Pappadou was downright worried about you, Ma'am, so I thought it would relieve his mind if I just moseyed up to find out how you were coming."

"Is he all right?" gasped Mrs. Pappadou. "Nothing awful happened?"

"Everything went smooth as syrup," said Jim. "And your Pa turned out to be his daughter's own Dad, Phil, a rough rider just like you. He performed like a regular old timer. You should be proud of him."

"Did he? Tell us!" cried Philippa.

"I'd tell you all about it right off," said Jim, "except I've been sort of shy on meals today. I was wondering if you folks have any plans about supper?"

"Coming up," cried Mary Carey, rummaging in the food boxes, "coming right up!"

Fifteen

The camp at Camas Creek suddenly seemed very different. Gloom and worry blew away like fog before a brisk wind. Even the rain seemed to have stopped, and a blurry glow behind the clouds showed where the moon was shining. Clem and José laughed and joked as they took care of the horses and piled up saddles and gear under tarps for the night. A crackling fire lit up Mary Carey's face with a cheerful glow as she cooked, wonderful smells of ham and coffee and beans and biscuits swirling around her.

Philippa cuddled happily in her sleeping bag beside her mother, who was questioning Jim about everything that had happened since he and Mr. Pappadou rode away into Myth Valley.

"We didn't have no trouble," said Jim. "It's no state

highway, that trail, but Mr. Pappadou took it like a good'un. Even that Gee Whizz pitch over the rocks above the scree didn't faze him. He let Freddy be in charge, which is the proper way. We got down into the valley before dark and found Jake Turpin right away. I reckon it's his collarbone and a couple of ribs—painful, but not all that serious. Better'n what he deserves, I'll say. He was sure talking different from the old Jake. According to him, the Angel Gabriel come down and knocked the devil clean out of him—'I ain't never goin' to sin no more,' he kept saying over and over. 'Honest,' he'd say, 'I see my transgressions . . . That there angel with his fiery wings . . . Don't let him come back! I'm a-goin' to be righteous from here on out . . .' I guess he was kind of delirious. We bound him up the best we could and got him onto Three Cheers. It took us most of the night to get down through the canyon to the ranch. Good thing I know that trail blindfold, because that's about the way we traveled after the moon set on us. Well, we finally got there—sure surprised Dad. But he was glad to see us when he found out who was hollerin'. And my Aunt Loretta, who keeps house for him, got up, rheumatism and all, and fixed us something to eat. So then we had a couple or three hours sleep before we started for town."

"Merciful goodness. You must be exhausted!" cried Mrs. Pappadou. "And Papa—I hope he doesn't become ill—so much exertion, so little sleep!"

"Don't worry about him, Ma'am," Jim reassured her. "He's been pert as a prairie dog all day. I sort of think he enjoyed himself. Anyway, he and my Dad had a real good talk coming in this morning in the truck. Dad had to lay in supplies for the roundup next week, so he brought us in. We fixed up a hay bed in the back for Jake. He was pretty uncomfortable by this time, as you can imagine, and still goin' on about the Angel Gabriel and how he's never goin' to sin no more—on and on and on. Crazy. It was a big relief to get him into the hospital and off our hands."

Mary Carey now began filling a row of plates with baked beans and slices of ham and biscuits almost too hot to touch.

"Come and get it!" she called.

"Not a moment too soon," said Jim. "Another three minutes and I'd have keeled right over dead of starvation."

"What about Three Cheers and Freddy and Black Magic?" asked Philippa, when everybody had settled down to supper. "What did you do with them?"

"Oh, I left them at the ranch," said Jim. "Simpson won't be needing them this late in the season and I can fetch them back sometime before the roundup. Anyhow, they've got it better over there than they ever do on this side of the mountains. That grass must have like vitamins in it or some kind of magic. It beats anything for the horses. Cattle do well, too, but horses! Myth Ranch is the place for horses!"

"Oh *dear!*" sighed Philippa. Then, after a long pause, she said, "Does Sadie live there?"

"Sadie?" said Jim. "Oh, you mean Sadie? Well, no.

The fact of the matter is, she's not living anyplace now."

"What do you mean?" Philippa was puzzled. "How can she not live someplace?"

"Because I had to shoot her, that's why," said Jim very seriously. "She doesn't live anyplace."

"*Jim!*" Mrs. Pappadou was shocked.

"I wouldn't have done it, only in self-defense, Ma'am," said Jim earnestly. "She'd have poisoned me in another week. Her cooking would have killed a full-grown moose, honest. It was a case of her or me."

"Jim, you shouldn't make such jokes!"

"It wasn't no joke!" Jim sounded as if his feelings were hurt. Clem had been listening with a peculiar look on his face.

"Jim Randell, you surprise me," he said in a reproachful tone. "Was that any way to treat Sadie after all she done for you? That game little girl who stood by you in many a close shave? Why there was a dozen times when I wouldn't have give a nickel for your chances if it hadn't been for Sadie. Yessir, I'm surprised at you!"

"Shucks," said Jim. "I didn't have any use for her anymore. Besides," he went on defensively, "she was mine, wasn't she? I'd like to know who had a better right to shoot her!"

"Mama, did he really?" Philippa didn't know whether to believe him or not. Of course it wasn't right to shoot people, but how lovely if Jim had stopped being married.

"Clem and Jim are joking," said Mrs. Pappadou, looking very disapproving. "It is not a funny sort of joke."

Clem glanced at Jim.

"Well, I'll tell you, Ma'am," he began, "the truth about Sadie is . . . How about it, Jim?" Jim looked embarrassed, but he nodded. Clem went on: "You see, a young feller in Jim's line of work runs a lot of risks. He's liable to get roped and hog-tied . . ."

"What do you mean? Who would do that to him?" said Mrs. Pappadou.

"What I mean, it's all these lady dudes come out here summers. They got one idea, to catch theirselves a cowboy and marry him. It comes from Westerns on TV, or maybe too many cigarette ads. Anyhow, they're a determined bunch, and Jim being reasonably good-looking, and bashful by nature—he got into some pretty ticklish situations. So I dropped into a dime store and bought him a wedding ring—a good hefty one you could spot half a mile away. That relieved him of a whole lot of pressure. But then there was questions. What was his wife like? Was she a cowgirl?—stuff like that. So he worked up Sadie, and the rest of us helped him out with stories about what a terror she was, ready to pull a gun on any other girl who so much as looked at Jim—and the like of that. Quite a character, Sadie was—added local color around the campfire evenings along with the singing—you know, real Western. Didn't you folks get to hear nothing about Sadie?"

"I did," said Philippa. "Oh Jim, you mean there really isn't any Sadie?"

"Nope," said Jim, still looking embarrassed.

"Oh boy!" cried Philippa, "am I glad!"

"You sound as if you had designs on him yourself," said Clem.

"Not *me*," said Philippa, "but . . ." She looked around to see if she could catch Mary Carey's eye to give her a wink, but Mary Carey was busy with the dishes. She didn't seem to be listening. Now when Mary Carey's big chance was here at last—why couldn't she pay attention?

"Well, I wouldn't set your heart on him if I was you," cautioned Clem, "because if he went so far as to get rid of Sadie, it must mean he's got somebody else in his sights."

"Is that true, Jim?" asked Philippa, her heart sinking.

Jim didn't say anything.

"Is it a real person?"

"Now, now, Philippa—it's time for bed, dear," interrupted Mrs. Pappadou. "I think Jim must be terribly exhausted, and I know all of us are, my goodness! But Papa is safe, so we can all have a good sleep tonight."

Philippa fell asleep the moment she had wriggled into her sleeping bag. Mrs. Pappadou stayed awake longer, but even she never knew what time Mary Carey came to bed.

They *really* made an early start the next morning. It was still dark when the horses clumped into camp, hobbles rattling, bells clanging, José cantering at their heels with whistles and shouts. As Philippa crawled out of her sleeping bag, the mountain tops glowed pink, but the shadows around the tents still lay deep and frosty blue. Br-r-r-r-r! Breakfast was hurried. After breakfast, instead of staying to watch the tents come down and the pack-horses be loaded, Philippa found that she and her mother were to start down at once with Clem.

"But I wanted to come with Jim and the packhorses!" wailed Philippa.

No. Papa would be expecting them. There was much to see to and they didn't need to wait. Mary Carey would wait—she still had the dishes to do and would finish rolling the beds. Clem led up Old Blue and a bay mare named Nora, saddled and ready to go.

"Can't I ride Cindy?" Philippa looked at Jim. "Nora's just a packhorse."

"Cindy's sort of rested up now, Phil. If you rode her to-day you might get into town sooner than you intended to, and then again you might not get there at all, if you know what I mean. Nora's all right. She's really a saddle horse—she's only pinch-hitting for a packhorse this trip. You'll like her. Let me give you a leg up."

So they started. Clem rode ahead and led Cindy.

Nora was an all-right horse, but there was no proud-ness in riding her. Philippa felt sad. The whole trip to town was sad anyway—riding down, down, down, away from the high meadows and the high air, watching the faraway peaks sink out of sight, the trail getting wider and dustier, the flowers taller and weedier, until the horses were clattering on a road, meeting cars, passing houses and motels and stores, and then there they were— back in the ordinary world at Mr. Simpson's.

So then they had to say good-bye to the horses. Mrs. Pappadou had saved sugar for Old Blue, and she made quite a speech of love and gratitude. Philippa gave Nora a pat, but she put her arms around Cindy's neck and buried her face in the silky black mane. It was bad enough to say good-bye to Cindy, but Cindy had been Rico's friend, and somehow it was like saying good-bye to Rico, too. Tear marks smudged the dust on Philippa's face.

Then a station wagon drove up and her Papa jumped out and hurried over to them.

"Papa, you look wonderful!" cried Mrs. Pappadou, standing back and viewing Mr. Pappadou with admiration. "After what you've been through, my goodness!"

Mr. Pappadou said he hadn't been through so much, but he looked pleased just the same. His big hat was more dented and dusty than it had been, and his shirt and jeans and riding boots, which before looked as if he'd dressed up in them, now just seemed to be clothes. He looked more as if he belonged, and as if he felt he belonged and was proud of it.

"I tell you, Mama," he said, "Myth Valley is a place you must see! If we can only get there before it is too late. You just cannot imagine such a beautiful place—the lake, like a jewel, the magnificent view of the mountain, and a feeling—I do not know how to say it—of being away, away out of the world. And the flowers, you simply cannot imagine the flowers! Do you know what I wish, Mama? If there would only be time to make a collection of all the flowers in Myth Valley, a scientific collection— and then for you to paint them, too—all of them. Then whatever happens, there will be a record."

"I could never, Papa . . ." Mrs. Pappadou began, but

just then a dusty truck drew up and a big man got out and walked toward them. He had white hair and a kind face with friendly lines in it.

"Oh, Mr. Randell," said Mr. Pappadou. "Please come and meet my wife, and my daughter, Philippa. This is Jim's father," he explained, and they all shook hands.

"Did you succeed, Mr. Randell?" Mr. Pappadou asked. Mr. Randell shook his head. He looked worried and sad.

"I am sorry. I am very sorry," said Mr. Pappadou. "It is certainly nothing less than a terrible crime."

"Well, I guess I've reached the end of my rope," said Mr. Randell. "I can't seem to think of another thing to try. I sure hate to break the news to Jim. Did he come down with you, Mrs. Pappadou?"

Mrs. Pappadou explained that Jim would come down a little later with the packtrain. Mr. Pappadou said that it would give him great pleasure if Mr. Randell would bring Jim and Clem and José back to the hotel for lunch when they came in. Mr. Randell thanked him and said that he'd be glad to throw their duffle into the back of his truck and bring that along, too.

As the Pappadous drove to the hotel, Mr. Pappadou told Mrs. Pappadou that Mr. Randell had been hoping against hope that he could come to some arrangement with the Universal Development Corporation which would make it possible for him to keep his ranch. But apparently that effort had failed.

"The Corporation has bought up all the land surrounding Myth Ranch," he said, "land that Mr. Randell has leased for many years as winter range for his cattle. Without it he cannot make the ranch pay. The Corporation refuses to renew these leases. They are deliberately squeezing him out so that he will have to sell his cattle, and then—inevitably—his ranch. He stood out against them until his leases expired, but now he has no choice. The ranch will have to go."

If Philippa didn't understand all of what Mr. Pappadou said, at least she understood the end of it. Mr. Randell was going to have to sell his ranch.

"Papa," said Philippa. "I know what. Why don't *you* buy Mr. Randell's ranch?"

"Why not, Papa?" said Mrs. Pappadou.

"Even if I could afford it," said Mr. Pappadou, "whatever I was willing to pay, the Corporation would offer more. I, Pappadou, cannot fight Universal Development Corporation all by myself. Besides, if Mr. Randell, who is a successful rancher, cannot make the ranch pay, what could I do with it, a businessman?"

"Couldn't you save Myth Valley?" asked Mrs. Pappadou.

Mr. Pappadou sighed and said it was impossible.

When they reached the hotel, Mrs. Pappadou wanted Philippa to go up to their room and change into her city clothes. But Philippa begged so hard to stay in her jeans and boots just for the rest of the day that her mother had to give in.

After a while Mr. Randell arrived with all their camp duffle and with Jim and Clem and José and Mary Carey. They all went into the hotel dining room for lunch.

Mr. Pappadou ordered the biggest and best lunch to try

to cheer everybody up, because except for Clem and José, nobody seemed very happy. Mary Carey wasn't exactly sad, but she appeared to have something on her mind. Finally, she said:

"Mr. Pappadou, if you got me a ticket on the plane tomorrow, can we change it? Because I'm not going."

"Not going?" cried Mrs. Pappadou. "Why Mary Carey, what do you mean? Not coming home with us?"

"Not right away," said Mary Carey. "Fact is, I've had the offer of a job. It's just a temporary job, but I thought I'd stay and take it."

"What kind of a job, Mary Carey?"

"Cook," said Mary Carey.

"Cook!" Mrs. Pappadou could scarcely believe her ears. "Why Mary Carey, you've never cooked in your whole life, not until we went camping."

"Well, this job is for a camp cook."

It appeared that Mr. Randell would be rounding up his cattle in a few days. He needed someone to cook for the outfit, and Mary Carey had applied.

"These boys tell me this young lady makes pretty good biscuits. And I reckon she knows one end of a can opener from the other. That's our minimum requirements— anything she can do beyond that will be so much gravy. Jim's Aunt Loretta, who keeps house for me at the ranch, always used to like to cook for the roundup, but she's got arthritis so bad now, I can't ask her to go. We'll take good care of the young lady, never fear."

"There's eyewitnesses to the fact," said Jim, winking at

Philippa, "that the young lady's a pretty good hand at taking care of herself."

Philippa knew he was thinking about the ford at Myth Creek, but she didn't laugh. She didn't feel a bit like laughing. Here was Mary Carey going on a roundup, seeing the ranch, going to Myth Valley, perhaps, camping and riding and learning to be a sure enough cowgirl, while she, Philippa, had to go back to the city to school, to life without Rico. It wasn't fair.

"What's the matter, Phil?" said Mary Carey. "Why the face?"

"Mama needs you at home—to make the machines work," pouted Philippa. People are pretty quick to think up something to say when they don't want to say what they are really thinking.

"I guess she can get along without me for a couple of weeks," laughed Mary Carey. "I'm not—you know—that indispensable!"

By the time they had finished lunch, it was quite late. But instead of doing something worthwhile, like going out to Mr. Simpson's to see the horses again, they had to spend their last precious afternoon doing dull things on lists. Mrs. Pappadou wanted to get her hair done, and she said she hadn't sent a postcard to a single soul or bought any presents to bring back from the trip. Mr. Pappadou had a lot of arrangements to make, about the car and the camping equipment, and so forth—he was very busy. So it was almost supper time before they were through, and by that time the whole afternoon was wasted.

"Camping is nice, but I must say a hot bath and clean sheets are nice, too," said Mrs. Pappadou cheerfully that night.

"If I had my sleeping bag here I wouldn't sleep in any old sheets," grumped Philippa. But she certainly did sleep—so hard that the next minute it was morning.

"Hurry, dear," said her mother.

Breakfast, and they were off to the airport. Mary Carey drove them in the station wagon and Jim came along to show her the way. Philippa tried not to think about the trailer that had trundled after them the last time they traveled in this station wagon. With Rico in it.

It was a hundred miles to the airport, but they were there in no time.

Good-bye. Good-bye, Jim. Yes, see you next summer. Come home soon, Mary Carey. Good-bye . . . Good-bye.

They climbed into the huge airliner. It roared and they were off.

Good-bye, mountains.

Oh, Rico! . . .

Sixteen

Myth Ranch
Sept—or is it Oct?
Gee, I've lost track.

Dear Folks:

Yours r'c'd and it's sure nice to know a person's missed. Also glad to hear from my Dad that all is A-O.K. at the Towers and that those Van Pottle creeps have moved out, esp the dog (if you can call that thing a dog). Great that the new tenants in that apt have four nice kids—what a break for you, Phil!

Well, I could write you a book about the roundup, but I guess it will have to wait—except to say it was just great (nobody died of indigestion, either, you'll be surprised to hear). The only thing, it was kind of sad— the last roundup at Myth Ranch after goodness knows how many years, you know.

Before I forget it, Jim says to tell you that Jake Turpin got out of the hospital and has gone to live near some niece in North Dakota. He was still telling anybody who'd listen how the Angel Gabriel came down and knocked the devil out of him. Mr. Randell and Jim both think Mr. Pappadou was smart not to turn him over to the Sheriff because he really does seem to have got religion and is harmless now if balmy, and besides, can you imagine Philippa trying to tell a jury what really happened?

Well, Phil—I hope you weren't too disappointed that our plan didn't work out—you know—the one where I was to marry a cowboy with a ranch. I'm sure sorry about that.

The funny thing is, though, it did sort of half work out—but not the half you were most interested in. Guess what? I really am going to marry a cowboy! The only thing is, he doesn't have a ranch.

Yes, it's Jim—believe it or not! Turned out I was that other girl he shot poor Sadie for. So, after a while, he got around to letting me in on the secret.

But maybe we will have a ranch someday, somehow, and in the meantime perhaps Cindy'll have a surprise for you when you all come out next summer—that is a MUST. If we are lucky, we can make it to Myth Valley before it is all spoiled.

I've written my folks about Jim and I—I hope you'll tell them you think it's O.K.

> *Love and kisses,*
> *Mary Carey*

P.S. Here's hoping you really do think it's O.K.?
P.S. again. Thought we'd get married pretty soon after the cattle are sold—might cheer Jim up, he's feeling sunk, poor guy. Buyer coming out Tuesday.

What exclamations and laments, what cheers and excitement, when *that* letter was read!

"Oh, I am so glad it is Jim!" cried Mrs. Pappadou. "Mary Carey could not have chosen a nicer young man. And I think for a girl like Mary Carey it is a good thing to live out West. Mary Carey needs a lot of wide open space."

"Cindy must be going to have a foal, that's what she means," cried Philippa.

Mr. Pappadou was thoughtful.

"It is too bad," he said, "it is just too bad. Mr. Randell is a good man, he has worked hard. But what can he do? How can one rancher stand up against a corporation like Universal Development? They call it progress, but I do not think it is the right kind of progress."

He sighed as he got up from the table, put on his hat and coat, and left for the office.

"Is today Tuesday?" cried Mr. Pappadou, bursting into the apartment that afternoon, an hour and a half early.

He threw his hat and coat on a chair, instead of hanging them up in the hall closet the way he usually did.

"Hi, Papa—" Philippa came cantering down the hall. "Guess what? The teacher read my composition out loud to the class. It was about Cindy." Her Papa didn't seem to hear her.

"Why yes, I think it is Tuesday—yes, of course, it is," said Mrs. Pappadou, surprised. "What's the matter, Papa?"

But Mr. Pappadou didn't even answer. He hurried into the living room and grabbed the telephone. He dialed once, looking at his watch.

"Operator, please," he said impatiently. "I wish to place a long-distance call. Yes. Person to person. I want

to speak to Mr. Dan Randell, Myth Ranch—no, no, M—
Y—T—H, that's right—at a place called Lariat . . . yes,
yes, I have the number." Mr. Pappadou gave the operator
an area code and seven numbers.

"Myth Ranch? Mr. Randell?" Philippa and her mother
looked at each other, astonished. But when they started
to ask questions, Mr. Pappadou only frowned at them and
shook his head, listening. He kept looking at his watch
and playing the piano with his fingers on the table.

Philippa was so excited at the idea of his talking to
Mr. Randell that she had to jump up and down on the
sofa, but very quietly so as not to miss a word.

The operator took a long time, but finally somebody answered.

"Hello," said Mr. Pappadou, "hello . . . Mr. Randell? This is Pappadou . . . Can you hear me? . . . Well, it's good to hear yours. That's right—I wish we were. Well, Mr. Randell, I called because I happened to hear something today I thought you ought to know. Tell me, have you sold your cattle yet? You say the man is there now? You've signed? . . . Och!" Mr. Pappadou struck the table with his hand. "So I am too late! . . . Well, but never mind. Will you ask this man if he will sell you back the cattle for what he agreed to pay you, plus . . . plus, say— ten percent? Please ask him now, while I wait . . . He is willing? . . . Good . . . Never mind, I will explain, and I will send you a check for that amount at once, airmail . . . O.K., O.K. Do with them? Keep them! . . . That's what I said . . . I'll explain. If what I heard today is true, and I think it is true, you do not need to sell your cattle. *You do not need to sell your ranch!*"

"Oh Mama!" Philippa forgot to be quiet. She jumped off the sofa and threw her arms around Mrs. Pappadou's neck and hugged her breathless.

"Yes . . . quiet, please, Philippa. Well, I'll tell you. I have a business friend downtown who knows a great deal about the Universal Development people. He says their whole enterprise is shaky. They're overextended, he says. Several of their biggest projects aren't paying off. That big artificial lake they have built out in the desert, the 'City of Venice' . . . well, it's leaking, and they've had some labor trouble—the Gondoliers' Union has been on strike since last spring. Then their 'Tropical Alaska' resort is in difficulties, too. The frostproof dome keeps cracking, and the valuable flamingos and chimpanzees and so forth, they catch cold and have to be hospitalized or replaced. Not to mention the palm trees. My friend says the whole enterprise is close to bankruptcy, and in any case, he knows for a fact that they are going to put their properties in your area up for sale, starting very soon . . . Yes

. . . yes, exactly . . . the lands you've been leasing for grazing. Yes, I know, you can't keep your cattle unless the new owner is willing to lease to you. Well, the new owner *will* be willing . . . I'm practically sure of it . . . Do I know who he is? Well, not exactly, but if it's who I think it will be, you have nothing to worry about . . . Yes, yes, I'll certainly keep in touch . . . Oh, and will you please give our felicitations to the young couple . . . We are delighted, simply delighted, all of us . . . O.K., sir . . . good-bye."

"Oh, Papa, tell us quickly!" cried Mrs. Pappadou when Mr. Pappadou had put down the telephone.

But Mr. Pappadou would not tell.

"We must wait, and hope, and keep our fingers crossed," he said.

Every afternoon after that Philippa rushed in from school to see if her mother had heard anything, and every night she was in the hall, waiting for her Papa.

But he just kept looking worried and saying—"Nothing yet. Nothing yet."

"I shall have to give up my painting lessons until something is settled," said Mrs. Pappadou. "I am so nervous I cannot concentrate."

Then one day, about a week later, Mr. Pappadou came home and it was clear that something had happened. He was in a funny state of mind—he seemed happy, but he seemed keyed up, too, like a man who has done something exciting, or even dangerous.

"Tell us, tell us!" cried Mrs. Pappadou and Philippa. "What about the ranch?"

"Everything is going to be all right. Universal Development Corporation has sold every foot of land it owned in Lariat," said Mr. Pappadou.

"Will the new owner lease the land to Mr. Randell?" asked Mrs. Pappadou, breathlessly.

"I forwarded Mr. Randell a lease by airmail today," said Mr. Pappadou. "The new owner will lease the land on the same terms as before."

"Hooray, hooray, hooray!" cried Philippa. She would have liked to do three cartwheels, one after another, like Mary Carey—but she didn't know how.

"Who is the new owner, Papa?" Mrs. Pappadou wanted to know.

"Well," said Mr. Pappadou, with a funny, half-happy, half-scared look on his face, "as a matter of fact, *you* are, Mama! You are the new owner. You now own twelve thousand two hundred and sixty-three acres of rangeland in Lariat, adjacent to the Myth Ranch, in the western foothills of the Myth Range."

"*Me!*" cried Mama. "My *goodness!*"

"I want you to understand, Mama," he went on seriously, "that this is not a small investment, and probably not a wise one. I am afraid it is speculative—not the sort of business I ever go into. It is probably costing us more than we can afford. But . . ."

"Who cares?" cried Philippa.

"*Me!*" repeated Mrs. Pappadou. "I own all that land?

All that grass, and flowers, and view of the mountains? And right next to Myth Ranch, too! I do not care what it cost—whatever it cost, it is worth it."

"The grazing fees from Mr. Randell will pay the taxes, I think," said Mr. Pappadou, sounding businesslike, "but for a return on the investment—I fear there will be none."

"What about saving the ranch for Mr. Randell and for Jim and Mary Carey? What about Myth Valley? What about our summers in the mountains—a place for a little house, perhaps, and Papa—the flowers . . . "

"What about HORSES!" cried Philippa.

Mr. Pappadou looked at them and smiled.

"I thought of those things," he said. "I thought we'd get a pretty good return on our investment after all."

Three days later, a big envelope arrived postmarked Indian Springs—a really huge envelope, so fat it took four airmail stamps to send it.

"From Mary Carey," said Mrs. Pappadou, recognizing the handwriting.

"Open it, open it!" cried Philippa.

Mrs. Pappadou opened it. Inside was a paper folded over and over. It opened out, fold after fold, until it was as big as a circus poster. They had to spread it out on the living room floor. When they got it all spread out, there was just one word printed on it in red letters two feet high!

Then way down at the bottom they saw something else in tiny writing:

Mr. and Mrs. Jim Randell.

"She's married!" exclaimed Mrs. Pappadou. "Isn't that wonderful!"

"She's got a ranch," cried Philippa, "isn't *that* wonderful! The plan worked! But oh dear, I just don't know—I really, really, really just don't *know* how I can wait for it to be next summer!"

Seventeen

Nothing much happened during that long winter. Except for one thing, Mr. Olympio's letter.

Of course the Pappadous felt it only right to let Mr. Olympio know about Rico, so Mr. Pappadou wrote him the whole story. Then, at the end of his letter, he wrote:

I hope you will not think, Mr. Olympio, that the sorrow of losing him makes us regret the gift of Rico. Nothing could be further from the truth. He gave Philippa and my wife and me, too, the greatest joy while we had him, and the joys we have found because of Rico will stay with us always.

"Does that sound right?" asked Mr. Pappadou. Mrs. Pappadou said it was beautifully put, and true, too.

"Papa, won't you please ask Mr. Olympio if he has seen Rico, or anybody else has?" said Philippa. "I just have to know if he got back. He *didn't* fly straight as an arrow home to his own mountains the way Mr. Olympio said he would, because I saw him at Myth Meadows the next day—the day Cindy was lost."

"I'll ask him if you like, dear," said Mr. Pappadou, "though I doubt if Mr. Olympio has time to look for animals as hard to see as Rico."

Mr. Olympio's answer, when it came, was disappointing. He wrote:

I have not been able to get to the mountains myself for several months. But when I received your letter I sent a member of my staff, a Mr. John Hermés, who is well acquainted with our mountains and mountain folk, to make careful inquiries among the villagers. His report was discouraging. The mountaineers told him that they have not sighted even one of the pegasid horses since Rico was captured, and they think now that Rico may have been the last of the breed. They say the dams are responsible. What they mean by this is that the roads, dams, and hydroelectric plants now being built in many formerly remote valleys of our mountains are making too much of a disturbance for these shy creatures. Some wild animals can live with man and tolerate his technol-

ogy, *while some cannot. I cannot be opposed to develop-*
ments which will bring prosperity to a poor people, yet I
can only mourn the cost.

In your fortunate land, you can afford everything.
You have room for your great industries to turn out
unheard-of manmade riches, yet room besides in which
to cherish those other riches which man cannot create,
but only destroy—the shy and precious treasure of the
wild.

"What does that mean?" asked Philippa.

"Something the Universal Development Corporation doesn't bother much about," said her father thoughtfully.

"But Rico?" urged Philippa. "If he didn't go back, what happened to him?"

"If Mr. Olympio cannot tell us," said Mr. Pappadou, "I really do not know who can."

Summer came at last. Mrs. Pappadou packed all their Western clothes in their camping duffle bags, Mr. Pappadou sent a telegram to Myth Ranch to tell Mary Carey and Jim what time to meet them at the airport, and they were off!

Philippa could hardly wait to get to Myth Ranch, but there was one thing that troubled her: Mary Carey's promise that she could pick any horse she wanted from the horses on the ranch. Philippa had been thinking about this promise and worrying about it all winter, because it was obvious that all the horses on the ranch belonged to Mr. Randell and to Jim. Mary Carey didn't have any horses of her own to give away.

But as it turned out, Philippa needn't have worried. Mary Carey had explained about her promise, and Jim and his father both said that it was fine with them — Philippa could have any horse on the ranch.

"I think you deserve to have a horse of your own, Phil," said Jim. "Go ahead and take your pick." This was generous of Jim, because he was pretty sure which one she'd pick — his Cindy, of course — there wasn't another horse on the ranch to beat Cindy, and Philippa knew it.

But Philippa patted Cindy's velvet nose and smoothed her slick black mane and said she'd decide later. She was waiting to see Cindy's foal.

"It'll be a couple of weeks yet," said Jim.

"Well, it'll be a couple of years before she can even begin to ride him," said Mary Carey, "and in the meantime she'll have to have something to get around on. What about Splash, Jim?"

Splash was a black appaloosa with a white rump splattered with black spots. He looked as if someone had thrown a whole pail of milk at him from behind. Besides his striking appearance, he had beautiful manners and beautiful gaits. Philippa loved him at once.

And Mrs. Pappadou was delighted to find Old Blue waiting for her at Myth Ranch. Jim had bought her from Simpson for Mrs. Pappadou's exclusive use. Old Blue became her constant companion, taking her wherever she wanted to go in search of flowers, and waiting for her patiently while she painted a picture, no matter how long it took.

Jim was busy helping with the construction of the Pappadous' house on Lost Creek, not far from where it runs out of the canyon. The Pappadous camped nearby, waiting for the house to be finished, though Philippa was so happy to be camping again, she didn't care if it was never finished.

After they had spent a week or so seeing Myth Ranch and riding around exploring their new land, Mr. Pappadou wanted to organize a pack trip into Myth Valley.

"This is what I have been waiting for," he said. But Philippa begged to stay until Cindy's foal was born.

"There are certainly enough flowers right here to keep you busy for a few days," said Mrs. Pappadou. There certainly were.

"I'll be glad to take you in any time you want to go," said Mr. Randell, "even if Jim's too busy. I've been wanting to go up there anyhow. There was a couple of Government men went in last month—hired horses from me for the trip. They were looking into the matter of putting the valley and the whole Myth Range into what they call the Wilderness System. If it goes through, and they say it's certain to, it'll mean the valley can't be developed or changed, just left the way it is, always, wild and hard to get to."

"That's wonderful news!" said Mr. Pappadou. "Even in the short glimpse I had of Myth Valley, I could see it is a very special place. It has a sort of magic."

"That's right," said Mr. Randell. "Most everybody feels

that way about it. Everybody, that is, except those developers who wanted to 'improve' it. You can't improve a place like Myth Valley—you can only spoil it."

Three mornings later Jim heard his father calling from the shed down by the corral where a big roomy stall had been fixed for Cindy. Jim came running.

"How about that?" said Mr. Randell, who was standing looking into the stall.

There beside Cindy stood the cutest, spriest, funniest wobbly-legged little creature that ever switched a stubby tail.

"Isn't that something!" said Mr. Randell.

It was a little filly. She had piebald markings of a most distinctive and beautiful silvery gray and white.

"I don't know as I ever saw a pinto that color," said Mr. Randell.

Jim moved his hand forward and gently stroked the little creature.

"I have, once," said Jim. He paused. "Do you know, Dad, I hardly think Black Magic sired that baby."

The moment Philippa saw the foal, her choice was made.

"That's not going to be any ordinary horse," said Mr. Randell. "You've got yourself something pretty special there, Phil."

"I know," said Philippa, with shining eyes.

"What you going to name her?"

Philippa named her Lyra.

Epilogue

*I*f you should drive out west one of these summers with your family, chances are you may stop at the beautiful big campsite at Indian Springs. If you do, try and persuade your folks to stay over a few days, long enough to take a trip into the mountains, really up, up above tree line, right to the meadows near the snow. You could hire some horses and a guide from Mr. Simpson—his horses are excellent, as you know. He still has Three Cheers and Chiquita and Freddy, and lots of others just as dependable.

Or perhaps—best of all—you could go to Myth Valley. It is a wilderness area now, which doesn't mean that people can't go there, just that nobody can build roads or hotels or parking lots or airports, and that it will be left always the way it is, remote and beautiful and wild. If you really wanted to go, the

best thing to do would be to drive all the way around to Lariat (the road is rough but passable) and make arrangements with Mr. Randell or Jim. If they are too busy to guide you in, maybe Mary Carey could go. She took up packing and can throw a diamond hitch as well as the average wrangler by now, and her camp cooking—well, her camp cooking is about the best thing Mary Carey ever took up.

I can't explain why it is so important for you to get really back up into the mountains—on horseback, or on your own two feet (like the Hartshornes, remember?). Really up, up to where the little alpine flowers shine among the rocks, where the wind off the snow fields cuts the sunny air—I can't possibly explain. You'll just have to go, and then you'll understand.

And when you get there, look at the mountains. Look carefully. If you have field glasses, train them on the high ledges, search the blue shadow along the glacier, the sweeping slopes of snow, the sky above the summit and the cloud-shadowed flanks of the distant peaks. You could see white goats on those dizzy ledges, or if you are really keen-eyed, a bighorn ram and his slender ewes. Cheers if you do! But they aren't what you are looking for. Neither are the mighty golden eagles sedately wheeling in the summit updrafts. It's another, even more splendid sight. Keep looking. If you are lucky you might—you just might—see something you will never forget, something so beautiful, so very glorious, you will dream about it all your life afterwards, yet scarcely believe in what you saw.

Good luck!

Typeset in Goudy Old Style by Parabola Books.
Production Co-ordinator: Rob Baker

All Parabola Books have sewn bindings
and are printed on acid-free paper.